SOGGY

"It did break."

Eddy Stone looked down at the upturned face of his cousin Millie. Wide eyes gazed back at him through a tangle of curls that tumbled past her dimpled cheeks and over the shoulders of her pink princess dress. She made a very sweet picture – apart from the twisted handlebars that she held in one hand, and the oily chain that dangled from the other.

"What do you mean, it did break?" said Eddy. "How could it just break? It's a bicycle."

"I did not break it." She bit her bottom lip. "But what would happen if somebody did?"

3

"Somebody," said Eddy, "would be in a lot of trouble."

The bottom lip began to tremble.

No, thought Eddy, *not more crying*. He had had quite enough of Millie's crying – a noise that was as loud as a police siren and as sharp as a lemon. In fact, he had had quite enough of Millie.

"So," Eddy added quickly, "it's a good job that you had nothing to do with it and aren't in trouble at all." He hoped that would be enough to stop the tears from coming.

The lip stiffened. It was going to be okay.

Or as okay as it could ever be with Millie around. Which was not very okay at all.

This was the first Christmas holiday that Eddy had spent in the little seaside town of Tidemark Bay, in the cottage that his parents had bought during the summer. He had been looking forward to playing outside in the snow and relaxing inside with the TV and his video games. The weather had ruined the first part with a week of grey skies and every kind of rain you could imagine, from drifting drizzle to torrential drenchings – so much that even the local ducks had taken shelter. And as for relaxing – Millie had soon put paid to that.

Eddy's Aunt Maureen and Uncle Ken had brought Millie with them to stay for the holidays, and the grown-ups had all agreed that what a four-and-three-quarter-year-old bundle of mischief really needed was her sensible eleven-and-a-half-year-old cousin Eddy to keep an eye on her and set her a good example.

Eddy had not agreed. Eddy had not even been asked.

Tonight, the grown-ups had decided that the best way of getting ready for Christmas was to practise having a good time, and they'd gone out for the evening.

"We're only down the road in the pub," said his dad. "You've got your phone if there's any problem."

So here he was, stuck with Millie and the job of entertaining and restraining her. Less than half his age, less than half his height, and more than twice as much menace as he could handle.

She was already losing interest in the bike. She dropped the chain onto the floor of the hall where they were standing, leaving an oily smudge on the carpet, then tossed the broken handlebars over her shoulder.

They looped through the air
and smacked into the ceiling
light, cracking the glass shade,
before clattering down onto the
hall table and sending a stack of
Christmas cards flying.

Eddy tried to be patient with
her. But Millie used up every scrap
of patience he had, and then came
back for more.

"Let's get these bits out of the
way," said Eddy with a sigh, as
he stooped to pick up the
bicycle chain. "And then I'd
better find the rest of the bike.
Can you remember where
you left it?"

"I know it was in
your bedroom," said
Millie helpfully.

"My bedroom?" said Eddy. "Why was it in my bedroom?"

"It looked tired," said Millie. "I thought it needed a rest. It was very hard work getting it up all your stairs."

Eddy set off to bring it back down. He noticed the long scratch on the wallpaper by the staircase.

"It is not there any more," said Millie. "Not after it fell out of the window."

"And how did it do that?" said Eddy, trying to sound calm.

"I don't know," said Millie. "It's just a big mystery."

"I see," said Eddy, struggling to scrape up a last bit of patience. "So it must have landed in the front garden."

He grabbed a torch from the hall stand. He could do without this. It was a filthy night outside. A fierce wind was howling in off the sea, lashing the pouring rain against the windows, and rattling through the letter box. He slipped the latch on the front door. The wind tugged it from his grasp and slammed it open.

"Why is wind?" asked Millie, perched on the stairs.

"Not now," said Eddy. He shielded his eyes with his hand and peered out into the murky evening.

He could see his bike splayed out on the front lawn.

One of the wheels was at a worrying angle, and the seat was stuck in the hole where the handlebars usually sat, but apart from that the damage didn't look too bad.

He pulled on a raincoat that was hanging by the front door and ran out into the garden. The wind saw its opportunity and with a sudden swirl blew water down his neck, up his sleeves, into his face, and over the sides of his shoes, soaking his socks in an instant.

"I hate rain," he said, getting a good mouthful of it in the process.

He grabbed the bike and turned to haul it back towards the house.

As he did so, he spotted something lying on the ground, halfway up the garden path. Something brown. Or brownish. It was hard to tell in the dark and wet. It looked like a soggy bit of cloth. Maybe one of the grown-ups had dropped a jumper or a scarf on their way out? It was soaked through, its surface matted together. He had better get it out of the rain.

He bent down to pick it up.

"Mew!" The sound was a hoarse whisper.

It jerked wearily away from him with a squelch.

"A cat!" said Eddy. It was only because of the mew

that he knew what it was. There was nothing furry or purry about it. With its hair slicked down by the rain, its tail trailing limply and water dripping from its drooping whiskers, it looked sodden and shivery and very sorry for itself.

"You can't stay out here. Let's get you inside – oh."

It was ahead of him, already staggering through the open doorway and into the light and warmth of the hallway.

"What is it?" Millie's voice piped up. "And is it allowed in here? It's dripping puddles on the carpet."

"It's okay. It's just a cat. And it's only a bit of water. That's not the end of the world," was Eddy's reply.

He was about to find out that every part of that reply was wrong. *Terribly wrong*.

HUNGRY

"I know you don't like it," said Eddy, "but we need to get you dry."

The cat squirmed beneath the towel that Eddy was using to rub it down.

"I have always wanted to have a cat," said Millie, bouncing up and down with excitement. "I will call him Mr Furrytummysnugglepaws and I will love him."

Eddy thought that being drenched in the rain was quite enough for a cat to suffer in one evening, without having to answer to such a ridiculous name as well. But he didn't say anything. He didn't want to upset her. And it didn't matter what she called this cat – it wouldn't be around for long. There was no sign of a collar or a name tag to tell them where it was from, but it must have wandered away from one of the houses nearby. Cats didn't just fall out of the sky. The weather was too horrible to do anything about it tonight, but in the morning he would set off to find the owner.

The cat now known as Mr Furrytummysnugglepaws wriggled out from under the towel. His fur, which had dried to a bright ginger, was fluffed up. He stood stiff and staring, and not at all snuggly. And when Millie reached out a hand to stroke him, he batted her away with a paw. And then lost his balance.

"Poor Mr Furrytummysnugglepaws," said Millie. "Don't be frightened."

"He needs to get used to us," said Eddy.

"I bet he will be friends with Horaceboris," said Millie, stamping off upstairs. "Everybody likes Horaceboris."

Horaceboris was her favourite cuddly toy. It had been knitted by her mother – Eddy's Aunt Maureen. Aunt Maureen knitted with a passion and a style that was all her own.

"Only beginners follow patterns," she would often say.

"Real knitters develop them." Eddy reckoned that Horaceboris had probably begun life as a pattern for a polar bear. Or a pelican. Or possibly a policeman. It was hard to tell once Aunt Maureen got going. However it had started, Horaceboris had developed into a lumpy creature of a smoky blue-grey colour, with a saggy bottom, a wide red mouth, boggling eyes and a shock of orange hair on the top of his head.

Millie loved Horaceboris. But she was wrong when she said that everybody else liked it too. When she thrust her cuddly toy towards Mr Furrytummysnugglepaws, the cat immediately backed away through the open door of the living room.

"Why did he do that?" said Millie.

"He's not settled in yet," said Eddy. "Let's go and sit quietly with him. We can watch TV."

The cat eyed them warily from the far corner of the room, looking about as relaxed as a choc ice on a radiator. Eddy reached for the TV remote and clicked the screen into life. An advert for a bottle of something to make men smell nicer at Christmas was just ending. The picture changed to a sleek grey cat prowling across a carpeted floor.

"Cats aren't just friends," a voice sighed over soft slinky music. The cat rubbed against a woman's legs. "They're family," the voice went on, "and your family deserves the best." The woman peeled open a sachet and tumbled glistening meaty chunks into a white bowl.

Mr Furrytummysnugglepaws walked unsteadily over to the television, reached up and patted the screen with a paw.

"Mew!" The sound came out more like a cough.

"He's saying that he's hungry," said Millie. "He saw the advert and now he wants his dinner. Who's a clever boy?"

The cat patted the screen again.

"I should have thought of that," said Eddy. "Come on. I think there's a slice of cold chicken in the fridge. He can have that."

They found a bowl in the kitchen cupboard, shredded the last of the chicken into it, and laid it down on the floor.

"There you are, Mr Furrytummysnugglepaws," said Millie. "Yum yum!"

The cat walked slowly round the bowl, eyeing it cautiously. Then he turned and sat his ginger bottom down on top of the food, and wiggled it around.

"Ewwwww!" said Millie. "What is he doing?"

"It's very odd," said Eddy. "I've never seen a cat do that before."

Mr Furrytummysnugglepaws sat still for a moment, as if waiting for something to happen. Then he lifted his bottom out of the bowl, turned round and pushed his face down into the pieces of chicken. When he raised his head again he was chewing slowly and uncertainly, like a child testing out a new vegetable.

A sudden blare of brass, beats and barking blasted into the kitchen from the living room.

"Come on," said Eddy. "*Hero Hound* is starting."
He and Millie hurried back and dived onto the sofa in front of the TV.

HERO HOUND was the latest hit action adventure series, the weekly tales of a doggy detective who thwarted dastardly villains and their schemes to take over the world. Once he had been an ordinary dog, but a mysterious radioactive flea collar had given him a handy selection of superpowers – from superspeed running to superhard claws, superloud barking to superpowered paws. His true identity was a mystery to everyone because of the mask that he wore across his eyes, but the pawprint logo on his cape and his cap was famous everywhere. He also had a neat line in rescuing puppies from raging rivers, burning buildings and cupboards under stairs.

And he wasn't just a hit on television. Eddy's mum and dad ran a business selling fancy-dress costumes for pets (well, nobody's parents are perfect), and the Hero Hound mask, cape and cap set was their biggest success – even more popular than the Sherlock Holmes waistcoat, pipe and deerstalker combo, or the full Queen Victoria (also available in extra-small sizes for guinea pigs). Hundreds of assorted dogs, from dachshund to Great Dane, were going to wake up on Christmas morning to find that, thanks to their owners, they would have to spend the day dressed in a mask, cape and cap with the famous pawprint logo – or at least, as much of the day as it took to tear the costume off and bury it in the garden when no one was watching.

Eddy and Millie sat silently as this week's thrilling **HERO HOUND** adventure unfolded – featuring a particularly bad baddy with a secret underwater base, a giant pet lizard, and a plan to steal Belgium. They weren't the only ones who were hooked. By the time they reached the first advert break, the cat had returned from the kitchen and was also staring at the screen.

"Mew!" Mr Furrytummysnugglepaws said huskily as another cat-food commercial came on – this time starring a not-quite-as-famous-as-she-used-to-be television chef, who took a deep sniff of the meat and jelly and told the world that it smelled so good she was tempted to try it herself.

"I bet," said Eddy.

"Mew!" the cat repeated, waving a paw towards the screen.

"He wants more food," said Millie.

"He can't still be hungry," said Eddy. "Not after all that chicken."

"Mew!" the cat insisted.

"He says he is," said Millie.

"Okay," said Eddy. "Let's see what else we can find in the kitchen."

✦ ✦ ✦

Forty-five minutes later, Hero Hound had defeated the villain and saved Belgium – along with a pair of very cute spaniel puppies that the giant pet lizard had been keeping for lunch. Now the superdog was using his superpowerful tongue to lap up gallons of the special beef-flavoured ice cream that was made for him by his owner, kindly old Mr Henderson (whose amusing short-sightedness meant that he had no idea at all about his dog's double life).

In the same forty-five minutes there had been three more breaks for adverts, each with an ad for cat food.

And with each cat-food advert, Mr
Furrytummysnugglepaws had mewed and mewed for
more dinner.

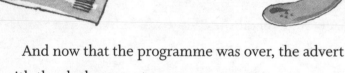

As well as the chicken,

he had eaten a tin of tuna,

a slice of ham,

the inside of a fish finger

and a leftover sausage.

And now that the programme was over, the advert
with the sleek grey cat was on once more.

"Mew!" said Mr Furrytummysnugglepaws. And
burped.

"There's something not right about that cat," said Eddy.

"Mew!"

"Rubbish!" said Millie. "He is my lovely Mr
Furrytummysnugglepaws and he is perfect. He must
still be hungry."

"Hungry?" said Eddy. "Look at him – his tummy's so
full it's scraping along the floor."

"I will get him something. *I* love you, Mr

Furrytummysnugglepaws. Come on, follow me."

Millie headed for the kitchen. The cat staggered after her, his trailing tum marking a faint furrow in the carpet.

Eddy heard the fridge door opening. And closing. Then a rattling as Millie searched the kitchen cupboard.

"There is a tin of rice pudding," she shouted. "Do cats like rice pudding?"

"He's had enough," said Eddy. "Just leave him."

"I will find out," Millie said, ignoring Eddy.

A moment later she came back into the front room.

"Your cat has been sick," she said. "It's all over the kitchen floor."

BOBBLY

"I know what cats like for breakfast," Eddy's Uncle Ken said loudly to the other members of the family, who were gathered round the kitchen table. "Mice Crispies!" he chuckled.

There was always laughter when Uncle Ken was talking. Usually it was Uncle Ken doing the laughing.

"Or a nice big bowl of mew-sli," said Eddy's dad. It was like this every time the two of them got together. They never stopped trying to top each other's terrible jokes.

"There's nothing left in the house that we can feed him," said Eddy. "He had it all last night. Until he gave it all back."

"What's brown and sticky?" said Uncle Ken.

20

"Not while we are having breakfast," said Aunt Maureen.

"What's wrong?" said Uncle Ken. "It's a stick. Brown and sticky – a stick."

Millie laughed. "That's funny," she said. "Because I thought it was going to be something horrid like poo."

"Thank you," said Aunt Maureen.

"You're welcome," Millie answered her mum. "For what?"

"I'm going out to see if I can find where the cat came from," said Eddy.

"Make sure you are home in half an hour," said Eddy's mum. "We have to get the last few costume orders in the post in time for Christmas. Your aunt and uncle have kindly offered to come and help pack them up, so we'll need you to look after little Millie."

"Again?" said Eddy.

"A bit of responsibility is good for you at your age," his mum replied.

"But it's supposed to be a holiday. You know, fun."

"It will be fun," said Millie. "We can play ponies – just like yesterday."

"I am not going to eat grass again," said Eddy. "It tastes disgusting."

"I quite like it," said Millie.

"You gave it a quick chew and spat it out when you thought I wasn't looking," said Eddy. "I saw you."

"I only said I *quite* like it," said Millie. "I quite like peas, too, and I do the same with them."

"What shall we do with you?" said Aunt Maureen with a sigh. No one said what they were thinking. They were all too polite. "It's ever so kind of you to look after her, Eddy."

"Yes," said Eddy. "I know. I'm off now."

"And don't forget your bobble hat," his aunt added.

"I don't think anyone could forget that hat," said Uncle Ken. "No matter how hard they tried."

The bobble hat was another of Aunt Maureen's special creations, knitted in stripes of red and green wool and decorated for Christmas by weaving in pieces of coloured ribbon, some plastic holly leaves, a strand of

battery-operated fairy lights, and strips of tinsel. Lots and lots of tinsel. There wasn't another one like it in the whole world – apart from the one that Aunt Maureen had made for Millie.

Eddy loved it. He liked the way people smiled when he wore it – though he drew the line at turning the fairy lights on. Not in the daytime. He pulled it down to keep his ears warm, and stomped off down the street.

The cold drizzle pricked his cheeks. He knocked on doors. But no one knew anything about a missing ginger cat. After ten minutes he reached the last house in the street. Clifftop Cottage. He didn't think it was even worth knocking there, because no cat would have lasted two minutes inside its high iron fence. Not with Brutus around.

Eddy was not sure what sort of dog Brutus was. He had once asked Brutus's owner, but the only reply he got was "a big one". The owner had also said that Brutus wouldn't harm a fly, but Eddy reckoned that was only because Brutus thought attacking flies was a waste of effort when there were so many larger things that would be much more fun to harm. Like neighbours.

He decided to give Clifftop Cottage a miss. He was

just tiptoeing quietly away to avoid disturbing Brutus, when his foot came down on a fallen leaf that was lying on the pavement. The leaf let out a sound – a faint crackle like a potato crisp being crunched by someone a whole street away. A sound that pricked Brutus's ears and brought him thundering and barking across the front lawn of Clifftop Cottage.

Wham! The great beast hurled himself against the front gate with a clang that made Eddy's teeth tingle.

"*Arf!*" He let out a bark that made Eddy's hair stand on end.

His owner always said this was just Brutus's way of being friendly. But Eddy didn't have any other friends who drooled uncontrollably when they saw him.

"*Arf!*" Eddy broke into a trot back down the street.

"*Arf! Arf!*" Further away and fainter, until he reached the safety of his own front door.

His mum was already in the hall with her coat on.

"Good," she said as he stepped inside. "Millie's playing on the computer in the front room. Lunch is in the fridge, I'm going to catch the others up, you have a lovely day."

"I won't," Eddy panted, but his mother was already

halfway down the front path. He peeled off his wet coat and hat. He would just have a minute or two of peace and quiet before he went to see what Millie was up to.

But the little girl appeared at the door of the front room.

"How did cats write before there were keyboards?" she said.

"What?" said Eddy.

"I mean, they couldn't hold pens in their paws, could they? Did they put them between their teeth, or did they just dip their paws in the ink and make big letters?"

"Cats can't write," said Eddy.

"Oh, ha ha," said Millie. "Of course they can."

"No, really," said Eddy. "They can't."

"Well, you had better tell that to Mr Furrytummysnugglepaws," said Millie. "He wants to know if we've got a hempi-something."

"What?" said Eddy.

"A humpi…perfi…oh, I can't remember now. Just come and see. He typed it on the computer."

CRAZY

Eddy followed Millie into the front room. The cat was sitting on the desk by the computer. There was a message on the screen.

I have come to your planet to give important information to your people._

Eddy read.

But my communications interface has malfunctioned. The hemispherical perforated diffusion baffle is worn out. It must be replaced. _

26

"Oh, right," Eddy said to Millie. "Cats from space. I bet this is your dad's idea, isn't it? You can't even say hemispherical perforated diffusion baffle, never mind spell it, but it's just the sort of thing that Uncle Ken would think was funny. Well nice try, ha ha, but you'll have to do better than this to trick me."

He expected Millie to break into giggles now that he had seen through the joke. But she didn't even smile.

"I so can say hupispurtical preferated division bottle and it wasn't me or my dad and you'd better read what the cat's typing now anyway, so there."

Eddy heard a slow tapping behind him. He looked round. His jaw dropped. The cat was picking out letters on the keyboard with his paw.

I need your help, _

the cat typed.

"See?"
said Millie.
"Told you."

"Can…you…

un…der…stand…what…I…am…say…ing?" Eddy said slowly.

"Yes…I…can," answered Millie.

"Not…you – I mean, not you," said Eddy. "Him."

Yes, _ the cat typed.

"Good," said Eddy. "Because I'd like to know what on Earth is going on. And off Earth, too, if you are really from another planet. And I'd also like to have a little sit-down. I thought there was something a bit odd about you last night, but this—" He ran out of words.

"Is everyone on your planet a cat?" said Millie.

This is not my true form, _ the cat typed. Our scientists built this tubeoid body for me so that my arrival would not cause undue alarm. We have been observing your home world – or minor planet Cz492gamma, as we know it – for several years. We have monitored your transmissions and gathered information by questioning one of your inhabitants. _

This brief message might have led Eddy to raise many intriguing topics of conversation.

Where was the cat from?

What did he mean about scientists building his body?

What was a tubeoid?

Why was Earth classified as a minor planet?

What transmissions had they seen?

Who was the inhabitant they had questioned?

And perhaps most intriguing of all, *how long* would it take for a video of a cat typing to get a million hits on the internet?

But Eddy asked none of these. His brain was quite busy enough being completely astonished. Instead, he just managed a small noise in his throat – like a hamster with a hiccup – as the cat continued.

We noted that the cat creature is the dominant species here and so... _

"What are domino speeches?" said Millie.

"Dominant species," Eddy managed to say. "He means the cats are in charge – the top dogs."

"Cats can't be dogs," said Millie.

"And they aren't in charge either," said Eddy. "Humans are."

We have observed that cats do whatever they wish, rest wherever and whenever they want, and ignore everything that you say to them – while you humans rush around all day, provide them with shelter, and obey the information boxes when they give you orders to feed them. _

"What information boxes?" asked Eddy. "What orders?"

The cat's paws dabbed at the keyboard. Last night, there were many orders for you to feed me on your information box. Too many for me, but I am not used to this strange tubeoid body with its primitive digestive system. _

Eddy suddenly twigged.

"You mean the cat-food adverts on TV?"

If that is what you call them. _

30

"But they are not orders to feed you. They are just trying to get us to buy things."

Your comment is noted, _ the cat typed.

This is crazy, thought Eddy. Could he really be talking to an alien – an alien in the shape of a cat? Well, if it wasn't an alien, it could only be a real cat with a wicked sense of humour that had suddenly learned how to type. And somehow that seemed even more unlikely.

"So what is this hemispherical perforated diffusion baffle that you need?" he asked.

It is a round piece of metal about as wide as your hand, with many small holes in it. _

"Like a small kitchen sieve," said Eddy. "But obviously not a kitchen sieve. I mean, whoever heard of anyone mending an alien spaceship with a kitchen sieve? Then again, whoever heard of anyone mending an alien spaceship at all? Hold on."

He rushed out of the room and rummaged in the cutlery drawer in the kitchen.

"Would this do?" he said when he returned. "It's a small kitchen sieve."

Possibly, _ the cat typed. But it will need to be covered with a damping baffle – it must be an organic material with a slight elasticity. _

"Like a woolly sock," said Eddy. "Wait here."

There was a pile of clean laundry in the kitchen, ready to be taken upstairs and put away. He found a grey school sock. He wouldn't be needing that for the holidays.

Back in the front room, he slipped the sock over the sieve. It fitted snugly. "It could have been made for the job," he said.

That might work, _ the cat typed.

Due to a planning error which has allowed this life form to evolve without thumbs, I am unable to grip anything. I will need your assistance to make the repair. When we step away from the device that I am now using, I will no longer be able to communicate with you, so pay careful attention. I will lead you to my space podule. You will not be able to spot it because it is behind a disguise shield. I will deactivate the shield and open the communications interface. You will replace the broken hemispherical perforated diffusion baffle. Follow. _

He jumped down from the computer desk and headed for the door.

"I can't leave you here on your own," Eddy said to Millie. "You had better come too."

"To see a spaceship! Try and stop me," said Millie. "Let's go!"

Like most parents, Eddy's and Millie's had warned them not to trust strangers. Unfortunately for everyone, they had never warned them to be especially sure not to trust strange aliens disguised as cats.

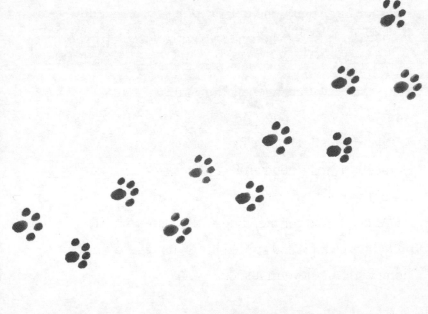

CRAFTY

"You'll need your coat," said Eddy.

"Who says you can tell me what to do?" said Millie.

"Your mum asked me to look after you," said Eddy. "And you would do what she told you to, wouldn't you?"

"Only if she told me to do what I wanted to do anyway. She worked that out ages ago. But it is cold outside so I do want to put my coat on. And my special Christmas hat."

She tugged her bobble hat over her head, told Horaceboris to be good and wait there for her, and raced out of the door.

"And you wait for me," Eddy called after her. He pulled his coat on and stuffed his own hat into a pocket, along with the sieve-in-a-sock.

35

The cat led them round to the back of the house, through a hole in the garden fence and across a small field to the woods that stood on the hill above Tidemark Bay. They pushed through some scrubby bushes and suddenly, right in front of them among the trees, they saw a toadstool. Its stem was almost white, its broad cap a smoky grey, speckled with large round dots of a darker grey colour. And it was almost as tall as a house.

It was like nothing on Earth.

It must be the disguise shield, thought Eddy. He was still wondering why the cat would choose a ridiculous disguise that wouldn't fool anybody, when suddenly there was no more ridiculous disguise for anybody not to be fooled by. The toadstool evaporated in a shimmer of light. And in its place he could see what must be the undisguised space podule.

Eddy had seen loads of books with pictures of what people thought alien spaceships might look like. He'd seen flying saucers and giant rockets and floating globes and fierce warcraft bristling with weapons. This podule looked nothing like any of them. It had a slightly wonky not-quite-round sort of shape – like a jellybean. Its outside was silver in colour and completely smooth all over. And it was almost as tall as a house.

The giant silver jellybean began to bulge on one side. The bulge grew larger, until it spat out a metal cube, about as big as a biscuit tin. The cube tumbled to the ground, and a lid popped open on its top. Inside, Eddy could see something round that was wrapped in a dark woven covering.

"What is it?" said Millie.

"This metal cube must be the communications interface," said Eddy. "And I think that round bit is the broken part that needs mending."

He pulled the sieve-in-a-sock from his coat pocket. He looked at the cat.

"Is that it?" he asked.

"Mew," said the cat. Which really wasn't any help at all.

Carefully and slowly, Eddy swapped the old part for his sieve-in-a-sock. The replacement was a bit smaller, but once it was in position, the rest of the metal cube shrank slightly around it, until the sieve was snugly in place. Then the lid closed again, and the communications interface rolled over to the cat.

"Do you think it will work?" said Eddy.

"I think it already has. Can you hear me?"

The sound of the new voice was not exactly in Eddy's ears. More between his ears. Right in the middle of his head. He looked at the cat.

"Yes," said Eddy. "How are you doing that?"

"Who are you talking to?" Millie said quietly.

"The cat," said Eddy.

"Why?"

"Because he is talking to us."

"Then why can't I hear him?"

"I don't know," said Eddy.

"The advanced brains of our species allow us to communicate by thought..." the cat was saying.

"I think I've got a bit of tinsel sticking in my ear," said Millie. She pulled off her bobble hat to sort it out.

"...but we need a communications interface," the cat went on, "to amplify the waves to get through your thick skulls so you can hear us."

"Ooohh," said Millie. "I think I can hear him now I've taken my hat off. Is that you, Mr Furrytummy-snugglepaws?"

"It's me," said the cat.

"Prove it," said Millie. "Say mew."

"Mew."

"Ooohh," said Millie again. "Who's a clever boy?"

"What do you think of the podule?" the cat asked.

"It's very shiny and – um." Eddy paused. "I don't know really, I've never seen anything like it before so I've got nothing to compare it to."

"It's the latest model," the cat communicated. "So fast that if you look round quickly after you've taken

39

off you can see yourself still on the ground about to leave. Want to take a look inside?"

Eddy hesitated. This was all very strange.

A small round hole, no bigger than a penny, appeared in the sleek silver skin of the ship, then grew larger and larger, like an opening mouth, until it was wide enough to clamber through.

"Last one in is a loser!" Millie shouted, making a run for the podule.

"Wait!" Eddy shouted. "Stay outside until I've—"

"Yes, Mum! Whatever you say!" Millie shouted back as she climbed in through the hole.

"And don't touch any knobs or levers!" he shouted at Millie's legs as she disappeared into the podule.

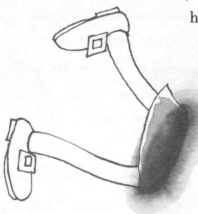

Eddy clambered in after her, hoping that she hadn't had time to break or fiddle with anything.

But there was nothing to touch. The inside of the podule was as smooth as the outside.

It felt slightly spongy – like a balloon filled with custard. And though it was silver on the outside, from the inside there were transparent windows, so they could see the woods all around them. The cat was still sitting among the trees, next to the metal cube that was his communications interface.

"Close door," said the cat.

"What?" said Eddy. "Wait a minute!"

But the opening that they had clambered in through had disappeared. They had been swallowed up.

"Scan complete." A voice rolled round the inside of the podule. "Physical functions and brain activity logged."

"Let us out of here," said Eddy.

"No," said the cat. "You know I am not from your world. My true identity must be kept secret from the rest of your kind. So you must be removed."

"Adjusting my shape for your comfort and safety," said the podule. Eddy felt the interior close around his legs and tilt him backwards, until he was seated and gripped tight.

"What's happening?" said Millie. "Is it a ride? Like at the fairground?"

"Sort of," said Eddy.

"And for your information," said the cat, "I am not Mr Furrytummysnugglepaws. How dare you insult me with that ridiculous name? I am Drax G'varglestarg, Ninth Level Agent of the Malvalian Pillaging Fleet. Now say goodbye – to all of this. You won't be seeing it ever again."

DOPEY

"Preparing for take-off," said the podule.

"Listen to me. We don't belong in here," said Eddy. "We're not your passengers."

"Correction," said the podule. "My orders specify the transportation of two tubeoid natives of minor planet Cz492gamma."

"So change the orders," said Eddy.

"My orders have a level nine authority. Checking your authority level. Your level is – zero. Orders remain in place. Please relax now and enjoy your journey."

"We're about to be sent to goodness knows where. How can I relax?" asked Eddy.

"Your brain scan indicates several ways to relax you," said the podule. "A calming colour…"

The podule's interior washed over with a soft pale blue.

"That wasn't what I meant," said Eddy.

"…soothing sound…"

Gentle violin music drifted through the interior.

"…friendly fragrance…"

The smell of warm cake hit his nostrils.

"…and a good dose of this sleeping gas…"

A wisp of yellow mist floated through the air.

"No!" said Eddy. "Wait!"

"Stop making such a fuss," the cat's voice sounded in Eddy's head. "Think of it as me doing you a favour. If you aren't here, you will be safe."

"Safe from what?" said Eddy, looking out of the podule window. The cat was sitting on top of the communications interface. "What are you going to do?"

Drax said nothing, but raised a front paw and waved up at the podule.

And then overbalanced.

"I hate this new body. It needs more legs," he said.

The podule suddenly shot into the air at tremendous speed. The Earth shrank to a tiny speck as the sky blurred from blue to black.

Eddy felt dizzy and dopey, as if his head had gone into orbit round the rest of his body. Everything outside was whizzing past in a woozy whoosh. Not that everything outside amounted to much. All around them was the great empty nothingness of outer space.

"It's boring," said Millie. Her voice was sleepy and slurred. "Can we go home now?"

"I don't think so," said Eddy. He didn't know what else to say.

"You'll look after me where we are going," said Millie, "won't you?"

"Of course," said Eddy. He couldn't quite manage to sound calm.

How far they travelled, how long or how fast, Eddy couldn't tell. He was struggling to stay awake as the sleeping gas took hold of him. There was nothing to see out of the podule window except thousands of distant stars.

Then suddenly out of the nothing ahead came a something, a dot that grew like a ball that had been hurled towards them, but was already too big to be a ball and getting bigger still, until it became a vast planet, striped and swirled with a cloak of grey and rust-brown clouds. Eddy thought he had seen pictures of it before, but the name refused to come into his giddy head.

The podule hurtled on, and behind the planet he saw a line of – what were they? Moons? He tried to see

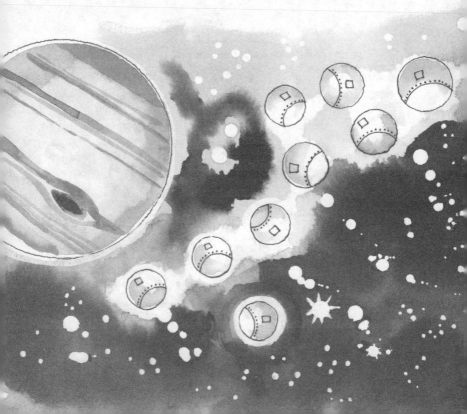

straight, to think straight, as the podule rushed
onwards. No – not moons. Spacecraft. Spacecraft
bigger than cities. The podule was heading directly for
the nearest one, right into a massive hole in its side
that opened up to swallow them with as little fuss as a
great whale gulping a microscopic shrimp. And as the
podule disappeared into the innards of the spacecraft,
the gas took hold and Eddy drifted into a deep sleep.

Drax G'varglestarg watched the podule disappear into the sky with its passengers. How easy it had been to trick the two Earth creatures and get rid of them. And now the Grand Control ship would be expecting his first mission report. He wasn't going to tell Grand Control about needing to repair the communications interface. Or about the mistake he had made when he had absent-mindedly sat on his food last night. Or the way he had overloaded his new digestive system. Grand Control didn't like to hear about problems – even after they had been solved. Grand Control wanted to be told that the mission was going to plan. Precisely to plan – no hitches, no glitches.

But he would have to mention the podule's disguise. It hadn't blended in to its surroundings at all. The mission briefing had said that the woods on this planet would be full of pixies and their toadstool houses, but there was no sign here of either. They would have to reprogram the shield. It would need a better disguise when they sent the podule back to pick him up after his mission was over.

He directed his thoughts into the communications interface.

"Agent Ginger Tom" (he was very careful not to pass on his thoughts about what a stupid code-name that was) "reporting to Malvalian Grand Control.

"I have successfully made a safe landing at the correct location on the target planet. The communications interface is operative and I will soon activate the mind-control program. I have adjusted to my new body.

"I must respectfully report that there is no evidence of pixie activity in this area, and request that you review the chosen disguise for the podule. The giant toadstool is not effective.

"I require further data. I have twice been asked to identify an individual known as 'Clever Boy'. I cannot find the answer in the mission briefing. Please advise.

"I have sent the podule back to you with two tubeoids for further study.

"Report ends."

He wasn't going to tell them that the two tubeoids in the podule knew that he was an alien, and up to something. That wasn't part of the mission plan. Anyway, if everything went smoothly, before Grand Control found that out, his work on this little wet planet would be finished. And so would the little wet planet.

HENRY

Eddy slept.

Strange visions swam through his head. He was floating through warm clammy air that tingled on his skin. Creatures surrounded him and peered at him curiously and poked and prodded at his limbs and gabbled about how tall he was and how much he weighed. It was just like meeting all his aunties at Christmas – except that his aunties weren't bright orange and their eyes didn't wave around on the end of long stalks, and when they prodded him it was with fingers with brightly varnished nails and not with twisted tentacles. And they didn't drip sticky slime – well, apart from Great Aunt Valerie and she didn't get invited round much any more.

And then there was brightness.

And a sour smell in his nose – like when Uncle Ken had put his socks in the oven to dry.

And something prodding him in the ribs.

And a voice.

"Who are you?"

"I'm trying to remember," Eddy mumbled in reply.

Uurggh. Eddy's head felt like someone had filled it with concrete. What had happened? He couldn't think. He forced his eyes open. There was green. A lot of green. But all blurred – like looking through someone else's spectacles.

The green began to float into focus. Leaves. Bushes. He was in a wide clearing with a circle of trees around it. It looked like the woods back home. Maybe that was where they were?

And then he saw the set of traffic lights, plonked down between two bushes. He didn't remember them being in the woods.

Or the purple sofa nearby. Or the grand piano. Or the little girl with tousled hair who was sitting up next to him.

Hang on – he did remember *her*. Millie! That's right, he had been with Millie. It was coming back to him now. There was a cat who wasn't a cat. And a journey through the sky. And a – oh, no.

"Are we on a spaceship?" he said.

"Afraid so." The voice came from behind him. A flat, hoarse voice. This must belong to the man who had prodded him in the ribs. Eddy turned and saw a figure with a wrinkled face, grey hair, and a long untidy beard. He was wearing tattered dark green trousers and a matching shirt. A uniform of some sort, Eddy thought.

Or what was left of it.

"Henry Handysides," said the man. "Private. 6060842." He held out his hand.

"Millie Stone," said Millie. "Four and three-quarters."

"And I'm her cousin Eddy," said Eddy. "Are you a soldier?"

"Army cook," said Henry.

"Best pastry in the regiment. I was known for it. Till I pulled guard duty on the wrong night. Just my flipping luck. 'Handysides,' says the Sergeant, 'lights have been seen in the woods where they didn't ought to be. Off you trot, and see what's what.' Next thing I know, some creature with orange tentacles is dragging me into his spacecraft, and I wake up here in the middle of all these trees. I never did like trees. Not even normal ones that stay still."

Eddy let the last remark go. He was already trying to take in enough new information without worrying about how trees might move.

"This is nothing like how I imagined the inside of a spaceship would be," Eddy said.

"Rubbish, isn't it?" said Henry. "Look at this. Green carpet everywhere instead of grass. Bits of furniture but no rooms. I think it's supposed to be just like our natural habitat."

"What do you mean?" said Eddy.

"It's sort of a zoo," said Henry.

"Ooh!" said Millie. "I like zoos. Are there hippotomopus…hoppotoppomus…hottopipamus… ephelants?"

"What are we doing at a zoo?" said Eddy.

"Not at," said Henry, gloomily. "In."

"In?" said Eddy.

"You'll see," said Henry. "Play my information, please, Ethel."

"And who is Ethel?" said Eddy.

"It's the name I gave the voice that talks to me – it belongs to the computer that does everything round here. It stands for Extra Terrestrial – oh, I can't remember the rest. I'm sure it meant something when I thought it up, but now she's just Ethel."

"Exhibit." Ethel's voice was brisk and bright. "A two-legged tubeoid from minor planet —"

"What is a tubeoid?" Eddy asked.

"Don't interrupt," Ethel interrupted.

"But I don't understand," Eddy interrupted back. "And this is supposed to be information, isn't it?"

"Oh, very well," said Ethel. "A tubeoid is a primitive creature that digests its food in a tube that runs through its body. Food is inserted at one end, and the waste comes out of the other."

"And how else are you supposed to eat?" said Eddy.

"Like properly evolved creatures do, of course," said

Ethel. "Spray your food with digestive juices while it is outside your body, suck up the goodness, and leave the disgusting mess that is left over where it belongs. Malvalians, for example, have juice tubes in their lower bodies, and sit on their meals to eat."

"That's what the cat did," said Millie.

"To continue," said Ethel. "Exhibit: a two-legged tubeoid from minor planet Cz492gamma. Population on home planet – large and increasing."

"And that's me," said Henry, sadly. "A two-legged tubeoid. Course they'll have to change that to say three two-legged tubeoids, now we're all together in this cage."

"What cage?" said Eddy. "I can't see a cage. No bars or fences. Just a clearing with trees all around it."

"They don't need bars," said Henry. "It's much cleverer than that. You see that stream over there? Just in front of where the trees begin?"

"Yes," said Eddy. The bank of the stream was clearly visible beyond the traffic lights.

"That stream goes round this clearing in a big circle. Like no stream I've ever seen before. Round and round, day after day, never getting anywhere. I know just how it feels…" He let out a long sigh, like a punctured football.

"And?" said Eddy.

"Just you take a step across it," said Henry. "You'll see."

"Okay," said Eddy. "Millie – you'd better stick with me." He waved at Henry. "See you later."

"It won't be much later," said Henry. "Don't get your hopes up."

Millie took hold of Eddy's hand. They walked together to the edge of the stream.

"I'm going to cross it now," said Eddy, "and find out what happens. You stay here."

"Why?" said Millie.

"Because I have to look after you. I want whatever happens to happen to me first." He dangled his right foot over the water. "Here goes." And he planted it down on the far bank.

"Go back to your place and stop being naughty!" It was Ethel.

"She sounds cross," said Millie.

"If that's what happens, it's not so bad," said Eddy. He lifted his left foot and stepped over the stream.

"If you don't go back, you won't get any pie!"

"That's quite bad," said Millie. "I'm hungry. I do want pie."

"Never mind that," said Eddy. "I'm going to see what's on the other side of those trees."

The treeline was just a few steps ahead of him now. He took a pace forward and – uuurgh. His head again. The trees seemed to swirl in front of him. Something must be wrong with his eyes. He blinked hard.

"Why did the trees do that?" asked Millie.

"Do what?" said Eddy.

"Move," said Millie. "Didn't you see?"

"I thought it was just in my head," said Eddy.

He took three steps forward. She was right. The trees definitely moved away from him.

What on Earth? thought Eddy. *Or rather, what not on Earth any more?*

He broke into a trot.

The trees speeded up.

He swerved to the right.

The trees followed.

He twisted. He turned. He made sudden stops and starts and spurts of speed.

Whatever he did, the trees moved to be exactly the same distance away from him.

He took a deep breath and ran at them, legs pumping.

The trees flowed away, as if he was chasing a wave down a beach.

"See what I mean?" said Henry. "Waste of time. You'll never reach them."

Eddy turned round. Henry was just a few paces behind him, standing by the stream. For all his effort, Eddy hadn't moved from its bank.

"I don't understand," said Eddy. "I was running. How can you run but not go anywhere?"

"Beats me," said Henry. "That's just how it is on that side of the stream. It's like the space stretches when you try to move into it."

"But we've got to get out of here," said Eddy. "There's an alien cat back on Earth who is going to do something bad, and we're the only ones who know about it."

"Good luck with that one," said Henry, with all the enthusiasm of a damp flannel. "I gave up trying to get out ages ago."

"How long have you been stuck in here?" said Eddy.

"I don't know," said Henry. "I lost count after the first three years. And that was ages ago. As you can see." He tugged at his long beard. "You had better get used to it. You're going to be here for the rest of your lives."

8
BOSSY

"Stuck here for the rest of our lives?" said Millie. "But that's after Christmas." Her bottom lip began to wobble. "We've got to be home for Christmas."

"I'm not going to give up trying to get out of here," said Eddy. "I promise." He stepped back across the stream to join the other two.

"That's better," said Ethel. "Don't let me catch you doing that again."

"Come on," said Henry, leading the way back to the centre of the clearing. "The pie will be here soon."

"Naughty boys don't get pie until they have earned it," said Ethel. "I've got some questions for you to answer."

"She's ever so bossy," said Millie.

A large black and white picture appeared in the air. The words *Gerald The Pixie* floated in front of a massive toadstool, its broad stem almost white, its cap a smoky grey speckled with large round dots of a darker grey. Jolly music struck up as a door in the toadstool's stalk opened and a figure stepped out. He had a tall cap, and long ears, and a pair of pointed shoes with rows of bells that jingled and jangled with every step. The figure broke into an annoyingly jaunty song.

"I've seen that toadstool before," said Eddy. "It's the disguise that the podule used."

"And I've seen this story before," said Henry. "Gerald thinks he has lost one of his socks. Looks everywhere for it. Until he realizes that he's put two socks on one foot by mistake. Load of rubbish."

"And now you've spoiled the ending," said Millie.

"Question," said Ethel. "When we showed you this information transmission before, you told us that this pixie is a common Earth creature in his house in a typical forest. Our Earth-landing site is in a typical forest, but there have been no observations of similar houses or creatures. Explain."

"That's silly," said Millie. "Everyone knows that pixies aren't rea—**MPPPPHH**!" Henry clapped his hand across her mouth.

"Really around at this time of year," said Henry. "If it's nearly Christmas, it's the middle of winter. The toadstools don't grow in winter, so the pixies live underground in burrows. Mostly asleep."

"Adding your answer to my central databank," said Ethel.

"Ow!" answered Henry, as Millie dug her teeth into his hand.

"What are you talking about?" said Eddy.

"One thing I learned in the army," whispered Henry, "is that you don't give information to the enemy. And anything with orange tentacles that drags me into outer space is definitely the enemy. So they've shown me lots of things off TV and asked me lots of questions about them, and I've told them lots of lies. I've said that everything is real – that's why they think all TV programmes are information transmissions. And that adverts give us orders about what to do."

"So that's why the cat thought we had to feed him every time there was a cat-food advert on TV," said Eddy.

"Stop that whispering," said Ethel. "Databank updated. We have intercepted a new information transmission. Watch and explain."

This time the pictures were in colour. And the theme song was one that Eddy and Millie recognized immediately – a blare of brass, beats and barking that announced the arrival of **HERO HOUND**.

"It's a dog," said Henry. "And um…" He hesitated. He hadn't seen the programme before and had no idea what would be coming up.

"And he has amazing superpowers," said Eddy.

"And he always beats baddies," added Millie.

"And absolutely nothing can stop him," said Eddy. "And I wish he was here. He'd get us out."

"Adding your answer to my central databank," said Ethel. "And now you may have your food."

A trolley trundled into view through the trees. As it drew near, Eddy saw that it was loaded with a large golden-crusted pie. Henry pulled plates and cutlery from the trolley, cut three slices and handed them round.

"I'm starving," said Millie. "I want pie."

"This is the moment I look forward to every day," said Henry. A filling of meaty chunks and rich dark gravy oozed across the plates. They each took a bite.

"And every day I'm disappointed," Henry said with his mouth full.

"I don't want pie," said Millie, spitting it out. "Pie's horrid."

Eddy chewed. It was an odd taste. It reminded him a bit of fish fingers. And Liquorice Allsorts. With a hint of toothpaste. And furniture polish.

"Ethel's very good at making it look right," said Henry. "She's seen pies in some of the films she has shown me. But I suppose the flavour is just guesswork. Still," he added glumly, "at least this one tastes better than yesterday's."

"You need to eat some pie," Eddy said to Millie. "Keep your strength up."

"But it's horrid," said Millie.

"It's just a bit different," said Eddy. He took a big mouthful. "Yum, yum," he lied.

He was hungry, he realized, as he swallowed. But then Ethel said something that made his appetite vanish.

"Your exhibit listing has been updated," said Ethel. "Here is the new version. Exhibit: three two-legged tubeoids from minor planet Cz492gamma. Assorted sizes. Population status on home planet – shortly to become extinct."

"Extinct?" said Eddy.

"What stinked?" said Millie.

"How can humans become extinct?" said Eddy. "Is this some kind of joke?"

"Ethel doesn't do jokes," said Henry. "No sense of humour."

"What do you mean, extinct?" said Eddy.

"Extinct," said Ethel. "Meaning – all gone. Wiped out. None left. Ended. Dead. Finished. Over."

"I know that," said Eddy. "What I want to know is how? And why? And come to that, when?"

"When the pillaging fleet removes all the water from the planet," said Ethel in a flat and emotionless voice.

"You're going to take all the water?" said Eddy in a voice that was not flat or emotionless at all.

"No more water!" said Millie. "That means no more baths! No more getting rained on! Oh – but no more puddles to stamp in. No more water pistols. No more—"

"No more anything," said Eddy. "Nothing on Earth can live with no water."

STICKY

"We've got to warn people back on Earth," said Eddy.

"Have you tried phoning them?" said Millie.

"We're on an alien ship in outer space," said Eddy. "You can't phone from outer space."

"I'm just being helpful," said Millie. "And I bet you haven't tried."

Can you phone people from outer space? thought Eddy. *It sounds unlikely, but...* He pulled his phone from his pocket and – no signal. *No, of course you can't phone people from outer space. It was a daft idea.*

He needed a great idea. And he needed it now. There was no time to lose. *What if...?* But nothing would come.

"Henry," he said. "You're the grown-up round here. You should be making the decisions. What do you think we should do?"

"Don't ask me," said Henry. "I haven't had to decide what to do in all the years I've been here. Or when I was in the army. I was just a private. Did what the officers told me to. Why don't we wait here and just see what happens?"

"Because if we wait here, we'll never find a way to warn Earth," said Eddy. "We can't just sit in this cage. We need to get out."

"We can't," said Henry. "And anyway, what's the point? We'll still be stuck on an alien spaceship. Where are we going to go to?"

"I haven't got as far as 'to'," said Eddy. "Just away. Away from this cage. It's a first step. That's got to be better than doing nothing. And then maybe we can find something that will be a second step."

"So how do you think we're going to get out of the cage?" said Henry. "You saw what happens as soon as you cross the stream."

"I don't know," said Eddy. He still didn't have any great ideas. Well, if he couldn't think of any great ideas, maybe he would just have to try some not-so-great ones.

"Ethel," he said. "You are good with questions. So. How can we get out of here?"

"That information is restricted to operatives ranked level seven and above," said Ethel. "Ask a different question."

"What's our level?" said Eddy. "How do we get to level seven?"

"You are an exhibit," said Ethel. "It is not possible for exhibits to reach any level. You are a zero. Ask a different question."

"This is no fun," said Millie. "I want to play a game."

"I haven't got time," said Eddy.

"You're mean," said Millie.

"I'm busy," said Eddy.

"Why?"

"Because," said Eddy. "Look, Ethel wanted another question to answer. You ask her one. You have always got lots."

That should keep Millie occupied, he thought, while he tried to come up with a way to escape.

"I do have lots," said Millie. "Lots and lots. Ethel, why are ponies?"

69

"Checking databanks," said Ethel. "Pony. Four-legged tubeoid found on minor planet Cz492gamma. Feeds on apples and peppermints…"

"What about the pie trolley?" Eddy said to Henry. "That gets in and out."

"No use," said Henry, glumly. "I followed it once. Over the stream and poof! Disappeared into thin air."

"I know *what* are ponies," said Millie. "I am four and three-quarters, thank you. I want to know *why* are ponies?"

"Checking databanks," said Ethel. "Life forms on minor planet Cz492gamma are believed to have developed from…"

"Boring," said Millie. "What is the best number?"

"Checking databanks," said Ethel. "Different numbers are considered lucky on different planets. For example, on Habathalor one is regarded as the only lucky number, because whenever two or more Habathalorians meet, the biggest eats the rest."

"I've got an idea," Eddy said to Henry. "We've only tried to escape one at a time. If two of us go off in different directions, maybe it will be too difficult for the trees to move both ways at once."

"I don't know," said Henry. "It doesn't sound very likely."

"Let's try it," said Eddy. "We can't just give up."

"Giving up is a lot less tiring," said Henry.

"Blah blah," said Millie. "I think seven is best, but my friend Sophie says three is nicer, but she's just wrong, isn't she?"

"In many places, three is considered…"

"…much worse than seven," said Millie. "Who invented cabbage? And why did they bother?"

"Let's go," said Eddy. He set off at a trot towards the trees. Henry began to stroll slowly off in the opposite direction. Eddy soon stepped across the stream. The trees retreated from him just like before.

"Anything?" he shouted over his shoulder to Henry.

"Hang on," said Henry. "I'm not there yet."

"Checking databanks," said Ethel. "I have no knowledge of cabbage."

"Lucky you," said Millie. "I wish I didn't. What is brown and sticky?"

"Checking databanks," said Ethel. "Listing all known brown objects in the universe, and all known sticky objects."

"I'm there now," shouted Henry. "And the trees are doing just the same as before. I told you it would be a waste of time."

"Well it was worth a try," shouted Eddy.

"It didn't work," shouted Henry. "So no, it wasn't."

"Back to the middle," said Eddy. "We need to think of something else."

"It's a stick," said Millie.

"No," said Ethel. "Stick does not appear in the databank list of objects that are sticky. List of known brown items complete. Number of entries approximately one trillion two hundred and twenty-six billion. List of known sticky items complete. Number of entries approximately three hundred and seventy-nine billion. Creating cross-reference grid to check for items which appear in both lists."

"It's a stick!" Millie repeated. "Brown and stick-y."

"Number of grid spaces required is approximately four hundred and seventy sextillion," said Ethel. "Cannot create grid. Insufficient computer memory available. Emptying temporary memory store. Ponies may be brown but not sticky. Peppermints may be sticky but not brown. Temporary memory emptied.

Insufficient computer memory available. Diverting memory circuits from other systems."

"What is she talking about?" Millie asked Eddy, as he returned to the middle of the clearing.

"She can't work out the answer to your question," said Eddie. "It's too big. She's saying that she has got to use bits of her brain that normally do other things."

"But it's just a joke," said Millie.

"I told you," said Henry. "She's got no sense of humour. Wouldn't know a joke if it crossed the road, walked up to her front door and shouted 'knock, knock'."

"Diverting memory from environmental systems," said Ethel. The light suddenly flickered and dimmed. "Diverting memory from communication systems. Diverty mimblery frump prejection symptoms," said Ethel.

"Prejection symptoms?" said Henry. "She's talking rubbish."

"The words must be getting mangled because she's shutting down her communication systems," said Eddy.

The trees began to shudder like the picture on a badly tuned television – just like the time Eddy's dad had climbed up on the roof to adjust the aerial with a gentle tap in just the right place with a hammer, and brought down half the chimney stack.

"And she's turning off her projection systems – that's what she was trying to say," said Eddy. "Look – the trees are all just projections. She's turning off the scenery."

The branches of all the trees suddenly vanished, leaving a forest of bare trunks.

"I did not break her," said Millie. "But what would happen if somebody did?"

"It might just give us our chance to get out of here," said Eddy.

The tree trunks suddenly exploded into a shimmer of brown dots that tumbled through the air for a moment and then disappeared. Instead of trees, Eddy could now see the outline of the cage that they were in. It was a broad circle of tall metal rods that stretched up to a high ceiling. There were wide gaps between the rods, and in the gaps was what looked like – nothing.

Nothing at all.

"System overload," said Ethel. "Sister mother load. Sit some other road."

A loud hum filled the air, like the swarming of ten million bees. And then a sudden silence. And the lights went out, plunging them into a deep blackness.

"I don't like it," said Millie.

"It will be okay," said Eddy, taking her hand and squeezing it. He hoped he was right.

"Ethel?" Henry's voice came out of the dark. "Are you alright?"

There was no answer. After a few seconds, the ceiling began to glow dimly, giving just enough light to see things nearby.

"That must be an emergency backup," said Eddy. "Let's find out if we can get out of here." He led the way across the stream, and took another step forward.

He waited to see if the metal rods that marked the edge of the cage would move away from him, just like the trees had done. But everything stayed still. Whatever strange trick had stopped them escaping before, it was no longer working its magic. He led Millie and Henry forward and out through a gap between two of the metal rods.

In the dim light from the ceiling they could just make out their surroundings. A huge open space stretched away around them, flat and grey and as big as ten football pitches. It was dotted with the shapes of more cages. The whole area was surrounded by dull metal walls, with dark doorways opening into them here and there. So this was the inside of an alien spaceship. Eddy had expected it to look exotic and exciting, but this was drab and dreary and about as exotic as an empty school playground on a wet Wednesday afternoon.

"Let's go," said Eddy. "We'll head for the wall over there and see if there's anything useful through those doorways."

"I reckon we'll need to be very, very lucky to get that far," said Henry. "Have you got a plan?"

"Yes," said Eddy. "I'm planning to be very, very lucky. Let's start by being careful. There are more zoo cages all around us – and whatever creatures were in them before, they're all on the loose now."

THURSDAY

They didn't notice it creeping up behind them. One moment they had almost reached the grey metal wall that they were heading for, moving stealthily in the dim light. The next moment there was a pittering pattering sound at their backs, and when they turned – there it was.

It was red and yellow, somewhere between a giant prawn and the biggest cockroach you could never wish to meet, with a leg at each corner of its body and six in the middle for good measure. As it scuttled towards them it reared up on its back legs. Now it was as tall as Millie. Long antennae waved in the air as its eyes swivelled on each side of its head. A head from which a pair of saw-toothed pincers stuck out. Pincers that were coming closer and closer.

Eddy started to shout, but his voice caught in his throat and came out in a strangled squawk like a sneezing budgie.

Henry managed to mutter a quiet, "Oh, great."

Millie's voice did better. A lot better. She let out a shriek that stopped the thing dead in its tracks. It began to rub its pincers together, making a sound like someone dropping marbles into a tin bucket.

Millie shrieked again.

"EEEEEEEEKKK!!!!"

The thing put its front legs to its chest and fiddled with a small metal device. A green light flashed on and the noise of the pincers was replaced by a voice: "That's a heck of a way to say hello, dollface. You're making my head rattle." Millie stopped shrieking.

"Now that's better," said the thing. "So, what's with the squealing, huh?"

"It's because you surprised us," said Eddy.

"And because you are scaly and scary and horrid," added Millie.

"Yeah? Well, where I come from we tell stories about soft squidgy creatures like you to frighten the kids. But you shouldn't be scared of me. In fact, I'd bet that I'm the only friend you've got in this place. Here's how I look at things." He stuck his eyes out on stalks and swivelled them wildly in opposite directions. "Heh! You like that? Just a little something I do to break the ice. The name's Thursday by the way. Thursday Cornflake."

"That's a silly name," said Millie.

"Is it? I have no idea. It's this TalkTheTalk translator." He tapped the metal device on his front.

"You have a translator?" said Eddy.

"What? You think everyone in the universe makes the same moo-mah noises as you? Normally the central control computer translates for everybody all over the ship at once, but it must be out of action right now."

"It did break," said Millie. "But I did not break it."

"I carry this little box because I often have

79

conversations in secret places that I don't want the computer to know about," said Thursday. "The TalkTheTalk speaks over thirty thousand languages like a native, and replaces strange and difficult names with familiar, fun and friendly words to provide a comforting experience for the listener. That's what it said on the box, anyways. My real name is –" he turned off the green light on the TalkTheTalk, rubbed his pincers together to make a noise like someone sawing through a metal pipe, and then turned the translator on again – "but I reckon you ain't got much chance of getting a sound like that out of that hole in the front of your face. So it's Thursday Cornflake to you, okay?"

"We're Eddy, Millie and Henry," said Eddy.

"And I guess you just broke out of one of the cages, right? Well – uh-oh…" Thursday broke off. "You hear that?" From somewhere nowhere near far enough away came the thump of galumphing footsteps and a deep snuffling snorting sound, like someone sucking the last drops of a milkshake up through a straw. "Unfortunately, that must also have just broken out."

"What is it?" said Eddy.

"I only know one thing that makes a noise like that.

And that thing, " said Thursday in a serious tone of voice, "is a Fluffy Wuffy Cushion Bunny."

"A what?" said Eddy.

Millie giggled.

"And – let me guess. My TalkTheTalk has just translated that name into something familiar, fun and friendly, hasn't it?" said Thursday.

"And cuddly," said Millie.

"Cuddly – no," said Thursday. "Big, stupid, clumsy – yes. Dangerous – definitely. And not something you want to meet. So I strongly suggest that we walk through that big open doorway in the wall over there –" he pointed with one of his middle legs – "and hide inside until it has gone away. And that we do it right now."

"Hang on," said Henry. "You want us to go in there with you when we've only just met? Have you never seen any scary movies?"

"You gotta make a choice," said Thursday. "Hide with your new friend, or stay here and meet that." The grunting snuffling snort got louder and nearer. "I understand that it's a tough choice. Unless, of course, you use whatever brain you have in those heads and think about it. I'm out of here. You decide." He ducked through the doorway.

The snuffling snort was sounding very close.

"I'm out of here, too," said Eddy. "Come on." He tugged on Millie's hand, and the three humans followed Thursday.

It was dark on the other side of the doorway. There were no lights working in the room that they had entered, and just a few steps inside the gloom was so deep that they could barely see where they were going.

"Over here!" It was Thursday's voice. Eddy, Millie and Henry followed the sound and found him tucked behind what appeared to be a large cupboard. They crouched beside him, out of sight of the doorway.

"So," Thursday said quietly, "everybody who ends up here on the Malvalian Grand Control ship has a story. What's yours?"

"We were kidnapped by a Malvalian disguised as a cat and sent here to the zoo," said Eddy.

"Zoo?" said Thursday. "You mean the cages, right? That ain't exactly a zoo. It's more a laboratory. The Malvalians keep creatures in there while they study them. They need to work out how to take over their brains when they want to steal from their planets. So what have you guys got that they are so interested in?"

"Just water," said Eddy. "The Malvalians want to take it all."

"Water is not *just* water," said Thursday. "It's special. One of the most valuable substances in the universe. You got a lot of it?"

"Oceans full," said Eddy.

"You gotta be kidding me. That's gotta be worth…I can't even imagine how much. No wonder the Malvalians want to take it. They will be able to sell it around the galaxy for gazillions. That's what I can't stand about them. They see something they want and they go out and grab it, no matter how many planets they ruin doing it."

"We've got to get a message back to our planet," said Eddy. "To warn them."

"I want to go home," said Millie. "It's horrid here."

"We'll see what we can do about that," said Thursday. "Me and a few of my friends took jobs on this spaceship. Me, I'm in waste disposal. It gets me into all sorts of places. And it's good cover for what we are really doing – which is whatever we can to stop the Malvalians' plans. Somebody has to save the planets; stand up for the little guys – even when the little guys are squidgy tubeoids. No offence, you understand."

"Communication and translation systems restored." It was Ethel's voice.

"She's back," Henry said happily.

"If she's turning back on, we need to get moving," said Thursday. "Before all the lights come on and all the doors get locked shut again."

A sudden snuffling snort sounded alarmingly close.

"On the other hand," said Thursday, "waiting till that Fluffy Wuffy Cushion Bunny has gone would increase our chances of staying healthy."

Another snuffle. Nearer this time. And then steps. Thumping in their direction.

"It must be right in the doorway," Eddy whispered. "Everyone keep very quiet, and very still." He took hold of Millie's hand again and held it tight.

And then he felt something wet. Something wet landing on his head and running slowly down the back of his neck. He reached up with his free hand to feel it and – URGGH. It was thick and sticky, like glue. More landed on the back of his hand. Whatever it was was dripping down on him. He wanted to get out of the way, but he didn't dare move in case he made a noise.

Heavy feet stomped just round the other side of the cupboard. There was a loud thump and crunch and a squeal of complaining metal. And then with a last snuffle and snort, the snuffling snorting thing trundled away.

"Okay," said Thursday. "Let's give that thing time to get clear, and then we'll be out of here. I know a guy who can help us. His place is not too far away. But we'll have to dodge the security robots. By now they'll be hunting for everything that escaped from the cages. I reckon we can make it without the robots spotting us just as long as it stays dark out there."

And then all the lights came back on.

"Environmental systems restored," said Ethel.

"Typical," said Henry. "Bang go our chances."

But nobody heard him.

All they could hear was Millie.

Looking up and screaming.

"EEEEEEEEEEEEEEEEEEKKKKKKKKKKKKK!!!!!!"

SLIMY

Eddy looked up to see what Millie was screaming at. What he saw made him jump back.

Tentacles. Dozens of them. Tangled orange tentacles dangling down like strands of limp seaweed and dripping thick slime. And above them an orange body like a beach ball, with two eyes on stalks staring blankly ahead. It was hanging on cords from the ceiling. And there were more of the creatures, a row of them stretching away across the room.

"EEEEEEEEEEEKKKKKKKKK!" Millie continued.

"Did she come with a volume switch?" said Thursday.

Millie finally ran out of breath.

"It's okay," said Thursday. "They're safe. This must be a Malvalian body store. You know how you've got a Malvalian on your planet disguised as a – what did you call it? Cab?"

"Cat," said Eddy.

"Yeah, that," said Thursday. "Well, what they did is build a cat body, and then transfer the Malvalian agent's brain into it. They keep the original Malvalian body here to put the brain back into when its owner comes home. Same with all the agents sent to different planets in different bodies. One of the bodies hanging here must be the Malvalian agent who is on your planet. Maybe even this one right above us. But don't worry about them – with no brains they aren't going to do anything to us."

"Except drip that goo," said Eddy. "I've got it in my hair and all over my hands. And I can't get it off." He rubbed his hands together. "It's like wearing a really icky pair of rubber gloves."

"We'll sort that out later, kid," said Thursday. "Right now we should get moving." Scuttling forward on his ten legs, he led the way round the cupboard towards the doorway where they had entered the room. In front of them was what until recently had been a sturdy metal table, but was now a tangle of twisted wreckage.

"Did the Fluffy Wuffy Cushion Bunny do that?" said Eddy.

"Like I told you," said Thursday, "big, stupid, clumsy and dange—"

He was interrupted by a loud clang. A huge steel slab slid into place across the doorway, shutting them in.

"Security restored." It was Ethel's voice. "All systems now fully operational again."

"Ethel," said Henry. "Nice to hear you again. I was worried about you. Now open the door and let us out of here, will you?"

"The Body Store is a restricted room," said Ethel. "The door can only be opened by operatives ranked level eight and above. Your level is zero. Request denied."

"But that level eight security business is for getting into the room," said Henry. "We want to get out. In fact, if we're level zeros, we shouldn't be in here at all. You need to make sure we leave, not lock us in. So come on, open up."

"Request denied," Ethel repeated.

"That's just brilliant, isn't it?" said Henry. "We escape from being locked up in the cage and end up being locked up in here. What's the point of that? We were better off where we started. At least it was comfortable."

"Hey, look," said Thursday. "There's a big button on the wall next to the door. Maybe pressing that will get us out." He walked over to the button and jabbed it with one of his legs.

But nothing happened.

This is not good, Eddy thought. If they couldn't get out of here they had no chance of getting a message back to Earth, and even less of getting themselves home.

"Come on!" Eddy said. "Open up!"

"Level nine command received," said Ethel.

There was a swish as gentle as the sound the front-room curtains made whenever Eddy's mum pushed them aside to check what the neighbours were up to. The huge metal door slid open.

"Everybody out," said Thursday.

"Wait," said Eddy. "If Ethel got a level nine command,

that must mean that something level nine is heading this way and wants to get in. Probably something with a lot of orange tentacles. Something that we need to avoid. Ethel – who gave you the command to open the door?"

"You did," said Ethel. "Analysis of mucus confirms your level nine status. Sir."

"What are mewkers?" said Millie.

"Posh word for snot," said Henry.

"It must be this stuff that I've got all over my hands," said Eddy. "That must be how the security system works. I suppose it makes sense – if you can change your body it's no use looking at faces, or fingerprints." He thought of the Malvalians' orange tentacles. "Especially if you haven't got any fingers." And their big round orange heads. "Or much of a face… Well, that's the first time I've ever used snot to open a door."

He headed through the open doorway.

And walked straight into a pair of robots.

One robot was short and stocky, the other tall and thin with a spiky head. Several things about them struck Eddy.

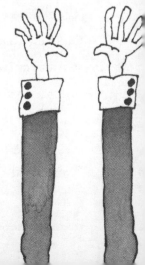

There was the way that they hovered a few inches from the ground and the glowing lights that pulsed in different colours around their bodies. But the thing that struck Eddy most of all was how they each swivelled a large gun in his direction.

"Security! Halt!" The stocky robot's voice was tinny and high-pitched. Not a sound that commanded immediate respect. But then you don't need much of a voice to get people to do what you tell them if you are pointing a big gun.

"Oh well," said Henry. "So much for being free. It wasn't really that great, though, was it? Just a lot of running away and getting locked in."

He held up his hands in surrender. Eddy did the same.

Was this it? Were they going to be thrown back into the cage? Or worse?

Eddy felt slime from his raised hands trickling slowly down his sleeves towards his elbows.

Slime.

Slime from the Malvalian's tentacles.

The level nine Malvalian.

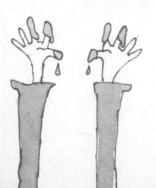

It worked on Ethel. So maybe…

He pushed his hands forward towards the robots.

"Oh," said Stocky. "Level nine. Apologies. Sir."

"We didn't recognize you in that body, sir," said Spiky. "Should have realized with you just coming out of the Body Store. Some sort of mission, is it, sir?"

"Yes," said Eddy. "But I can't tell you about it. And first I've got to deal with these three creatures who escaped during the computer glitch. I'm just taking them back to – um – where they came from. Over there." He wafted a hand in the general direction of somewhere else.

"Is assistance required?" said Stocky. "We're on round-up duty ourselves."

"I can manage on my own, thanks," said Eddy. "They are not much trouble."

"Oh, go on," said Spiky. "Let us help. Look, I've got this. It's new." He pushed a long probe out of the end of his arm and prodded Stocky with it. Electricity arced and crackled across Stocky's chest. "It's brilliant for getting things to go where you want them to."

"That really hurt," said Stocky. "Just watch it, Mr Look At Me I've Got An Upgrade." He swung an arm and bashed Spiky on the shoulder, leaving a dent in his metal skin.

"Oi," said Spiky. "Mind the new paint job. Anyway, you're only jealous." He prodded Stocky again.

"Jealous!" said Stocky. "What have I got to be jealous about? You may have your new probe, but you still haven't got anything half as cool as this." A panel in his body opened, and a whirring circular saw slid out.

"We'll just be on our way now," said Eddy, leaving plenty of room as he stepped around the two robots. Millie, Henry and Thursday followed him.

Behind them they heard the two voices carry on.

"Put it away," said Spiky. "We've all seen it before and it's boring."

"One more prod from you and we'll see how boring it is," said Stocky. The whirring got faster.

"Ow!"

"Ow!"

They had made it, Eddy thought. Escaped from the Body Store. Escaped from the Security Robots. Of course, they were still on an alien ship in outer space with no idea how to get home or even send a warning, but at least they were making progress.

"What are we doing now?" said Millie.

"I made a call back there," said Thursday, as they hurried away from the squabbling robots. "The guy I know. He's expecting us."

"A call?" said Eddy. "How?"

Thursday waggled his antennae.

"You think these are just for decoration?"

"This guy we're seeing," said Eddy. "Can he get us out of here?"

"Kid, if hc can't," said Thursday, "nobody can."

"That's not exactly a yes, is it?" said Eddy. "What if the nobody part is right and we can't get out of here. Then what will we do?"

TEDDY

"I'm hungry," said Millie, as Thursday steered the group away from the Malvalian Body Store. "And I want a drink," she added, as they passed through an opening in the wall and into a wide corridor.

"I'm sorry," said Eddy. "You'll just have to hang on for a bit. Right now we're trying to get off this spaceship."

"And my legs are tired," said Millie, as they tramped down the corridor. "Are we there yet?"

"Nearly," said Thursday, as they passed a long window that opened onto...

"Ooh! What's that?" said Millie.

"That, kid, is a space dock," said Thursday. "Where smaller spacecraft come in and out of this ship. It connects to the main traffic lanes that run through the place. And right next to it..." They reached a metal door set into the wall of the corridor. "We're here."

"What is it?" said Millie.

"It's a cafe," said Thursday. "The friend we're meeting, he runs this place. It can get a little lively in here sometimes. So stick close to me, stay cool, and everything should be okay."

He pushed the door open.

A sweet and sweaty smell hit their nostrils like a steaming compost heap. The air was filled with noisy chatter, and a jangle that sounded like someone was attacking a harp with a tin bucket while burping out a beat. Eddy guessed this must be some sort of galactic music.

They stepped inside. The noise stopped dead. Unfortunately, the smell carried on.

The room was packed with strange creatures large and small. Things that crawled and hopped and scuttled and slithered. Things furry, scaly, smooth and feathered, and one that looked like a giant marshmallow on legs.

"What are they all doing on this spaceship?" said Eddy.

"The work," said Thursday. "They keep the space dock going. If there's one thing Malvalians don't like, it's making an effort. They've got a saying – 'If a job's worth doing, don't bother asking me.'"

"I like it," said Henry. "Very good advice. I'll remember that one."

"Come with me," said Thursday. There was a long bar counter on the far side of the room. He led the way towards it.

Eyes followed them as they crossed the floor.

"Okay. That's just weird," said Eddy.

"Hey," said Thursday. "That ain't polite. Whoever owns those eyes, pick them up off the floor and put them away."

"Sorry," a voice grunted. A hairy creature reached out two long arms, retrieved the eyes and stuck them back into its head.

"And there's my guy," said Thursday, pointing to what appeared to be a large teddy bear standing behind the counter. "Hey! Boss!"

"He's cute," said Millie. "Can I cuddle him?"

"Don't be fooled by appearances,"

said Thursday. "He's a vicious fighter. He needs to be to keep this place under control on a fun night."

"Listen up, everybody," the Boss shouted. "These guys are my guests. And they are okay. So don't give them any trouble, understood? Now come on, you're here to enjoy yourselves."

There was a rumble of voices, and then the whole room let rip again.

"I saved you a space," said the Boss, pointing them to four empty stools at the end of the counter. They sat down between a giant green woodlouse and a pink jellyfish as big as a fridge.

"Something to eat?" said the Boss. "On the house."

"Yes, please," said Millie. "I'm starving."

"Got any pies?" said Henry.

"Never heard of them," said the Boss. "But we've some fresh sandworms. Delicious."

"Not for me," said Henry. "Can't stand foreign food."

"We don't really eat worms," said Eddy, trying to be polite.

"I do," said Millie. "My friend Sophie dared me and I did swallow nearly half a whole one. They taste much less horrid than spiders."

The Boss reached under the counter, pulled out a bowl and plonked it down in front of Millie. It smelled of vinegar and wet wellington boots.

"One worms," he said. "Enjoy."

They were fat and pale and looked quite like sausages. Until they started wriggling.

"Oh," said Millie. "I do like them, but I think I will save them for later, thank you."

"What's happening?" Eddy asked Thursday. "I thought your friend was going to help us escape."

"Take it easy," said Thursday. "It's all a matter of timing."

Eddy looked round the room. Everywhere, strange alien creatures were dipping tentacles and fronds and pipes into bowls of squirming worms and bugs in jelly, squirting out digestive juices and sucking up the goodness. And from all of them wafted steamy stinks and a stew of smells.

"I just remembered something," said Millie. She fished in the folds of her pink princess dress, and pulled the something out. "Jammy toast. Left over from breakfast. Yesterday. Want a bite?"

"After it has been in your pocket all day?" said Eddy. "No thanks." *I'd rather take my chances with the worms*, he thought.

"Okay," said Millie. She crammed the slice into her mouth.

"Oh, really," the giant green woodlouse muttered. "That's disgusting."

The muttering spread round the room.

"Eurrgh! It put something into the hole in its head.

In front of everyone!"

"How revolting!"

"I think I'm going to regurgitate."

The air filled with loud complaints. But not loud enough to block out the sound of a small explosion, and a clang as the back door of the cafe clattered to the floor in a puff of smoke.

"Nobody move," said a tinny, high-pitched voice.

Everyone in the cafe froze.

Through the door came a short and stocky robot, with a bent circular saw sticking halfway out of its scorch-marked chest. It was followed by a second robot with a spiky head and a limp probe dangling from the end of a mangled arm.

"It's the two we saw before," Eddy said to Thursday. "What do you think is going on?"

"Let's just sit tight," said Thursday.

"Everybody put your hands on your heads nice and slowly," said Stocky.

A grumble ran round the cafe.

"Well, if you haven't got hands, put your tentacles or pincers or whatever else you've got on top of your heads instead. Okay?"

From the back of the room came a single squeak.

"And if you haven't got a head, just put all your wriggly bits where we can see them."

"Are we clear on that?" added Spiky. "And all sitting nice and tight? Good. We're looking for three escaped tubeoids. We got a call to say that they are somewhere in this joint. One of them is pretending to be a level nine Malvalian in disguise. And we don't care for being fooled like that."

"I always thought there was something phoney about him," said Stocky.

"Oh, yeah, right," said Spiky. "What was it you said to him back there when you were so suspicious? Oh, I remember – 'Apologies. Sir.' Doesn't sound very suspicious does it, Stumpylumps?"

"Call me that again and I'll break more than your probe," said Stocky.

"Someone told them we were here," said Eddy. "This is terrible. We'll never escape now. Or warn people back on Earth."

"I just knew getting out of that cage was all a waste of time," said Henry.

"But I want to go home," said Millie.

"I can't believe it." Thursday turned to the Boss. "You betrayed us."

"Nothing personal," said the Boss. "I'm just an honest guy who obeys the law."

"I thought you were my friend!" shouted Thursday. "But you're just a sneaky RAT!"

Before the Boss could answer, there was a yell from across the room.

"Hey! What do you call this muck?" The owner of the voice was a purple frog-faced creature. He was clutching a large bowl. "I ordered fly soup. Waiter – there's no flies in my soup!"

He hurled the bowl through the air. It flew in a graceful arc, and whacked Spiky full in the face.

The robot turned, half-blinded as soup trickled into his eyes.

"Who did that?" he snarled.

And then it all kicked off.

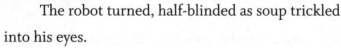

Plates, bowls, tables, chairs, and many of the smaller diners were hurled through the air. Spiky and Stocky were swallowed up in a writhing mass of fighting bodies.

WORM
BURGER
4 ZILLS

9 ZILLS

"And now we run," said Thursday.

"Thanks, Boss. That all worked a treat."

"For you, any time," said the Boss. "Besides, just look at this great fight." And he leaped off the bar into the middle of it.

Eddy, Millie, Henry and Thursday ran out through the wrecked back door. It led into the space dock. A shiny jellybean-shaped podule glinted under the overhead lights.

"You said it worked a treat," said Eddy. "Was that all planned?"

"Of course," said Thursday. "I told the Boss to call security. And he set up the frogoid with the soup to cause trouble when I said 'rat'. He came in right on cue."

"So what happens next?" said Eddy.

Thursday pointed to the podule.

"Security robots don't travel to emergency calls on foot. This shiny little beauty is their top-of-the-range double-engined souped-up space vehicle. And while the robots are tied up in that little diversion we created, your level nine clearance means it will be a piece of cake for you to steal this baby, take it out of this space dock and pilot it back to your home planet. So what do you think happens next?"

"Stealing is very naughty," said Millie.

"It certainly is, kid," said Thursday. "But I won't tell if you don't."

"Let's do it," said Eddy.

FARTY

"So how do we get into this thing?" said Eddy. He put his hand on the side of the podule.

"Oh my goodness," an excited voice came from the podule. "You're a level nine. What an honour. What can I do for you, sir?"

"We need a ride," said Eddy.

"You've got it!" The wall of the podule opened in a wide O. The travellers piled into its deep black interior.

"A level nine!" the podule repeated. "I am going to take extra special care of you and make sure that everything is just exactly how you want it. So – what about this colour? Security likes black, but I say dull, dull, dull! Shall we try something more cheerful?"

The inside of the podule changed to a warm purple.

"Can you do wallpaper with ponies on it?" said Millie.

"Of course," said the podule. "I just need to scan my databanks to find out what 'ponies' is."

"No you don't," said Eddy. "You need to get going."

"And fast," said Henry. "Look."

Eddy glanced out of the podule window. The robots must have escaped from the fight, and were coming their way.

There was a loud banging on the outside of the podule.

"Get out of there!" shouted Spiky.

"He's only a level three," said the podule. "So it's your call. Do you want me to let him in?"

"Absolutely not," said Eddy. "Just go."

"Sure thing," said the podule. "How about some music to relax you before take-off?"

"Go now!" said Eddy.

"The robot is getting a big gun out," said Millie. "He's pointing it at us."

"Would you like me to calculate how much damage the blast from his weapon will do to my hull?" said the podule. "And to you?"

"No," said Eddy. "Please hurry up."

"Are you sitting comfortably?"

"Yes!" yelled Eddy. "Go!"

"Then I'll begin."

"Too late!" said Henry. "He's going to – wow!"

Before he got to the second "w" they had shot out of the space dock and were hurtling away from the Malvalian ship and into empty space.

Eddy looked out of the window. He could see the ship that they had escaped from, and behind it a line of gigantic spheres. He counted ten, twelve of them. He had a dim memory of seeing them before.

"What are those?" he said.

"The Malvalian pillaging fleet," said Thursday. "The Grand Control ship at the front – that's where we were. And cargo ships behind it, all ready to fill up. Thirteen of them. The Malvalian's lucky number."

"And that planet they're near to," Eddy added, "with the stripes of grey and brown clouds. I've seen that in my *Book of Space*. That's Jupiter."

"It's simply great that you know where we are," said the podule. "And I hope you don't mind if I ask if you also know where you want to go."

"Earth," said Eddy. "Quickly."

"Earth?" said the podule. "I'm afraid I can't say that I know that one."

"The Malvalians don't call it that," said Henry. "To them it's minor planet Cz4 – oh, I can't remember."

"It's the third planet from the Sun," said Eddy, remembering what it said in his *Book of Space*.

"The Sun?" said the podule. "Is that the little star in middle of this system?"

"That's the one," said Eddy.

"Then you mean minor planet Cz492gamma."

"That's it," said Henry. "Cz492gamma. I should have been able to remember that. I must have heard Ethel say it a thousand times. You know, if I'd had a pound for every time she called it that – well, it wouldn't have been any use, would it, because there was nowhere to spend money in that cage."

"Let's just make sure we've got this right," said the podule. "Is this the place?"

A three-dimensional image of Earth appeared in

the middle of the cabin.

"That's it," said Eddy. "The Blue Planet."

"You're from the Blue Planet?" said Thursday. "You mean it ain't just a myth that space travellers tell each other late at night? Well I'll be – the Blue Planet. The Malvalians actually found it."

"It didn't need finding," said Eddy. "We were already living on it."

"Yeah, but who knew?"

"We did. Us humans. Or don't we count?"

"Hey, kid," said Thursday. "I'm on your side, remember?"

"I've plotted a course to our destination," said the podule. "It's just a short hop across this solar system. We'll be cruising at a comfortable one point five times the speed of light…"

"Hang on," said Eddy. "Nothing can travel faster than light."

"Tell that to the guys who built me," said the podule. "We'll be at our destination in a very short while, so I hope you enjoy the trip and have fun floating around in the reduced gravity."

Eddy felt a low rumble from the podule's engines.

There was no sensation of speed, but outside the windows the billion white stars that were scattered across the dark sky suddenly blurred into soft dabs of rainbow colours. Eddy floated slowly out of his seat.

"Whee!" shouted Millie as she drifted past him, turning slow somersaults. "This is brilliant! Why is space so big?"

"It just is," said Eddy.

"But how did it all get there?"

"I don't know," said Eddy. "And you need to stop asking me so many questions."

"Okay," said Millie. "Why?"

"Because I need to think about what to do when we get back to Earth."

"No you don't," said Henry. "You've already said

what we have to do. We report the alien invasion to the authorities and let them deal with the problem."

"I hope it's going to be as simple as that," said Eddy. "This whole thing feels like too much for me to cope with at the moment."

"You need to relax," said Henry. "Let me show you what I used to do to in the zoo when I wanted to take my mind off my worries." He put his left hand under his shirt, reached up into his right armpit, and squeezed down with his right arm.

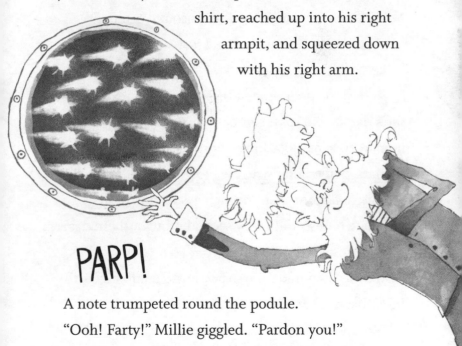

PARP!

A note trumpeted round the podule.

"Ooh! Farty!" Millie giggled. "Pardon you!"

"Farty!" said Henry. "Charming! Well, alright, I suppose it is – but just you listen to this." His arm moved up and down, and the familiar notes of the national anthem filled the air.

"That's impressive," said Eddy.

"I've got dozens of tunes I can do," said Henry. "Hours and hours I spent practising while I was stuck in that cage. Days and days. It was better than just wasting all that time, eh?"

He parped out a brisk marching tune.

"Let me try," said Eddy. But no sound came.

"You've got to get your hand just right," said Henry. "Like this…"

And so the podule sped through the far reaches of the solar system, past sights never seen before by human eyes, past clashing asteroids and the dry surface of Mars, while Eddy struggled to get a note out of his armpit, and Henry ran through a selection of his favourite tunes. And every second brought them nearer to an unsuspecting…

"Earth!" shouted Thursday. "That's got to be Earth! Just look at all that blue!"

EARTHY

"Agent Ginger Tom reporting to Malvalian Grand Control. Events are proceeding according to plan. Mind control has been established over the inhabitants of the Tidemark Bay target area. Cats have been recruited as guards and lookouts for the operation. Construction project has begun. Report ends."

It was a very simple report for what was turning out to be a very simple mission, Drax thought to himself. He had recorded his message on the communications interface, the interface had transmitted it across the town, and it had taken just a few hours to hypnotize everyone in Tidemark Bay. They were now completely under the control of his voice. A smooth operation from start to finish.

Not everything was quite as expected, though. By observing the town, and listening to conversations, he had discovered that some of the information that was logged in the mission databank was not correct. Carpet, for example, was not indoor grass. Bicycles were not an old-fashioned form of punishment. And the long perforated rolls of soft paper that were so often seen in adverts were not for writing on after all, but had a use so disgusting that it made him shudder to think about it.

He had not told Grand Control about these errors. Grand Control did not like errors. And anyway, what could it matter? The planet would very soon be dust. And then there would be no grass, no bicycles, and nothing for the paper to wipe.

He was also disappointed in the cats. They would be fine as guards. A promise of better food was all it took to persuade them, and sharp eyes, sharp teeth and sharp claws were a good combination. But they were very dull beasts. They had almost nothing to talk about. Half of the very few words that they used were to do with eating. And nearly all the others were the names of small furry things that ran away when they were chased, or small feathery things that flew away. All very boring.

But perhaps that was for the best. There was always a chance when you put on a new body that it came with impulses and instincts that started to take you over. Other agents had told him about missions in which they could not stop themselves behaving just like the creatures that they were disguised as. He couldn't imagine having a problem like that with this body. Cats were far too simple for that.

And now, Drax thought, he would just stretch out and have a little nap.

"Reducing speed," said the podule. "Entering atmosphere. Landing co-ordinates required."

"I don't know about co-ordinates," said Eddy. "We need Tidemark Bay."

"And I don't know about Tidemark Bay," said the podule. "I need co-ordinates."

"It's a little place," said Eddy, "near the coast. With lots of woods around it."

"I'm afraid that's not getting us very far, sir," said the podule. "Let's try to narrow it down. Looking at the planet, would you say that you want to aim for a blue bit or a brown bit?"

"Brown bit," said Eddy. "Show me that picture of the planet again."

"Will do," said the podule. The three-dimensional image pinged back into view.

"It's in this part," said Eddy, pointing out a familiar coastline. "Zoom in on this bit."

Step by step, Eddy homed in on Tidemark Bay.

"We'd better land somewhere just outside town," said Eddy. "We don't know what's going on in there." He pointed to the map. "There's a big wood here, between Tidemark Bay and the next town – Saltburn Sands. Can you get us down safely in the middle of it?"

"Can I?" said the podule. "Can a Tragalian Hypermonkey crack drindlenuts with its ears?"

Eddy said nothing. He was trying to picture just what a Tragalian Hypermonkey might be. And so were the others.

"The answer is yes, okay? They are famous for it," said the podule, after a long silence. "And my answer is yes, too. I *can* land safely in the middle of the wood. Just watch me."

Out of the window, Eddy could just see the coast, a brown edge against the blue sea. As they hurtled down towards it, he started to pick out towns, then roads, then rooftops, then…

"This brown stuff we're heading for," said the podule. "Is it hard or soft?"

"Hard," said Eddy. "You need to brake."

They plummeted down, towards the tops of the highest trees.

"Brake!" shouted Eddy. "It's too fast!"

Streaking past the treetops.

"Look out!" shouted Eddy. "We're going to—"

And then they were still. Suddenly, softly, as easily as taking the last step on the stairs; no more plummeting or streaking or whooshing, just tree trunks and bushes and a woodland floor around them.

"I hope you weren't going to say crash," said the podule. "Anyone would think this was your first landing."

"Land," said Eddy. "I was going to say land. We level nines are used to that sort of thing. Course we are. And we're right in the middle of the wood. That should stop us from being spotted."

"Don't worry about anyone seeing me," said the podule. "I can switch on the disguise shield."

"That's good," said Eddy. "As long as the disguise is not a very tall grey and white toadstool."

"Let me check the databank for the choice of disguises for use on this planet," said the podule. "It's coming up with just one option and that is – oh."

"A very tall grey and white toadstool?" said Eddy.

"Was that just a lucky guess?" said the podule.

"Forget the disguise," said Eddy. "I think that an undisguised giant metal jellybean looks a bit less weird than the toadstool. We've got a world to warn – so let everybody out now."

"Everybody?" said the podule. "If you say so."

There was a gentle hum as a round doorway opened in the cabin wall.

And then a loud crash as something large and heavy blundered out of the back of the podule.

"Look!" shouted Millie. "It's a real live Horaceboris!"

Eddy stuck his head out of the doorway. The thing that had come out of the back of the podule really did look just like Millie's favourite cuddly toy, Horaceboris. At least, like Millie's favourite cuddly toy would have looked if it had been ten times bigger in every direction and twenty times bigger round its bottom. It was about as large and shapely as a school football team in a sack, with a saggy grey-blue body, a wide red mouth, boggling eyes and a shock of untidy orange hair on top of its head.

Thursday scuttled across the podule on his ten legs and got to the doorway just in time to catch sight of the creature's bulging behind as it shambled into the shadows among the trees.

"Oh, no," he said. "Please don't tell me that was what I think it was."

"That depends," said the podule, "on what it is that you are thinking of. There is an extremely good chance that you are wrong because, of all the millions of things you could have chosen to think of, only one of them is what it is."

"A Fluffy Wuffy Cushion Bunny," said Thursday glumly.

"Well, my!" said the podule. "Everyone is winning the guessing game today."

"The owner of the most dangerous backside in the galaxy," said Thursday. "They don't mean to be bad. They aren't clever enough for that. They just like plonking down on things and squashing them."

"It was in the hold," said the podule. "The security robots captured it after it escaped from its cage. We were just about to take it back when we got the call to head to the cafe."

"And now it's crashing around on Earth," said Eddy.

"You did tell me to let everyone out," said the podule.

"I didn't know that everyone included that," said Eddy.

Through the open podule door he heard the sound of thumping footsteps heading into the distance, followed by a crunching crackling noise as the Fluffy Wuffy Cushion Bunny's broad behind flumped down, and a tall, thin bush suddenly began a new life as a short, wide bush.

"We'll have to worry about it later," said Eddy. "There's no time now. We've got a planet to save."

THIRSTY

Eddy led the way out of the podule.

"Hat on, please, Millie. It's cold out here," he said, as he pulled his own tinselly bobble hat over his head. "And stay here by the podule. Don't wander off."

"Can I have a drink? I'm very thirsty," said Millie. "And very hungry."

"You just need to wait a bit longer," said Eddy.

Thursday's ten feet scuttled round the clearing as he took a look at his new surroundings.

"So," he said, "this is the planet we're here to save."

"This is it," said Henry. "Home." He stood quietly among the trees, taking deep gulps of air. His breath turned into clouds of white vapour, lit by the low winter sun. "It has been a long time. All those years I was locked up. You know, I never thought I would see Earth again."

Henry kneeled down and ran his fingers across the woodland floor, stirring up a mixture of fallen leaves, pine needles and damp soil.

"Oh – now my hands are all mucky," he said. "I'd forgotten how grubby it is. And how wet. The knees of my trousers are soaked through."

"If the Malvalians get their way, it will soon all be dried out and dead," said Eddy. "We need to warn someone."

He fished in his jacket pocket and pulled out his phone.

"And now we're back on Earth, we can," he said. "If I can get a signal."

He took a dozen steps away from the podule, holding the phone up and checking its display. "Ah, that's better."

"Who are you going to call?" said Thursday.

"There's a place you can ring that has a list of everybody's phone numbers," said Eddy. "I'm sure they'll be able to tell me who I need to speak to."

He punched the buttons on his phone. His sticky fingers left smears of alien goo on the keyboard. There was a brief ring and...

"Enquiries," said a voice. "How can I help you?"

"Hello? I need to speak to someone who is in charge."

"You'll have to ring back in half an hour." The voice crackled in his ear. "The supervisor's on her lunch break."

"Not in charge of you," Eddy explained. "In charge of the country."

"I need a name, please, caller."

"The government. The head of the army. Air traffic control. I don't know," said Eddy. "Who is the right person to warn when there's an alien invasion and they are going to steal all the water?"

"Alien invasion?" said the voice.

"Yes," said Eddy. "I've got to tell someone."

"Then you'll be wanting the Alien Invasion Hotline," said the voice. "I'll just check the number."

"Really?" said Eddy. "There's a hotline?"

"No," said the voice. "Of course there isn't. I suppose this is one of those prank calls, isn't it? Are you recording this? So you can play it out on some radio programme and make me sound stupid?"

"No," said Eddy.

"Anyone else you would like me to look up while we're at it?" said the voice. "Miss Anna Conder at the zoo? Or her friends Ken Guru and Ray Nosseros? Some people think those are funny, too."

"You don't understand," said Eddy.

But the line went dead.

"She hung up," said Eddy.

"Are you surprised?" said Henry. "Aliens pinching all the water. I mean, *I* think it sounds pretty unbelievable and *I* know it's true."

"Emergency services," said Eddy. "They'll have to do something." He punched the number pad again.

"Emergency." The phone at the other end had barely rung before the voice cut in. "Which service do you require?"

"All of them," said Eddy.

"I can only connect you to one of them," said the voice.

"Please try to stay calm and tell me – what is the nature of your emergency?"

"It's a space alien," said Eddy.

"You should be ashamed of yourself, young man," said the voice. "There are people ringing with real problems, and you come on and waste my time like this. Are your parents there—?"

"Oh, forget it," said Eddy, ending the call.

"What is happening?" said Millie, wandering up to them.

"They won't listen," said Eddy.

"When people won't listen to me," said Millie, "I find it helps to roll around on the floor screaming and shouting. They soon change their mind."

"That won't work this time," said Eddy. "We're going to have to find some evidence to show people. Maybe if we go into Tidemark Bay there will be something happening. Something we can photograph and then – wait a minute. What's that in your hand?"

"Nothing," said Millie, putting her hands behind her back.

"Show me," said Eddy. She brought her hands out to the front again. Empty.

"See," she said. "Told you."

"You dropped this, kid," said Thursday. He held up a white cylinder, the size of a small cup, with a metal lid on top.

"Where did you get that?" said Eddy.

"I found it," said Millie. "In the back of the podule. I went to see if there were any more real live giant cuddlies in there but there were not. Only that."

"Well, well," said Thursday, "this could be very helpful."

"Why," said Eddy. "What is inside it?"

"Not what," said Thursday. "Who. You see these marks on the lid? They spell out the name Professor Blubblubblabblubblubblubblap. This is a hover vehicle for a Liquoid."

"A what?" said Eddy.

"A Liquoid is a creature with a body that's made entirely of clear fluid. They come from the liquid planet Ploop. These guys have the most brilliant scientific brains in the galaxy. That's why the Malvalians kidnap them and force them to work on new ideas and inventions. I've met a couple of Liquoids before on the spaceship, and they hate the

Malvalians for it. The Prof here must have been trying to hover out of the place when the computer systems were down, and got caught by the security robots. And my guess is he'll be happy to help us."

He unscrewed the lid of the hover vehicle. "Hey, Professor…oh. It's empty."

"I did not drink it," said a familiar small voice. "But what would happen if somebody did?"

LOVELY

"How are you feeling?" said Eddy.

"My head is a bit wonky," Millie answered.

"I hope you aren't going to be ill," said Eddy. "Don't you know you should never drink anything if you don't know what it is?"

"Or who it is," said Thursday.

"I told you I was very thirsty," said Millie. "And it just tasted like water."

"It's the Professor I feel sorry for," said Thursday. "What a terrible way to go – swallowed by a tubeoid. Just revolting. No offence."

They had almost reached the sign in the road that marked the edge of the town of Tidemark Bay. A cold wind whipped drizzling rain into the faces of Eddy, Millie and Henry as they walked along the pavement.

Thursday was keeping out of sight in the long grass at its edge. There was no point alarming the locals – not yet, anyway. Not until they had proof that an alien plot was taking place on their doorstep.

With a whir of wheels and the *tching!* of a bell, a cyclist came towards them.

"Lovely day!" he shouted as he passed them. "And everything nice and normal."

"You call this lovely?" Eddy shouted back. "It's freezing and wet and horrible." But the man had disappeared round the bend. "That was odd," said Eddy. "And why did he say everything was nice and normal?"

"Because everything *is* nice and normal," said Henry. "And it's a lovely day."

"Okay," said Eddy. "Let's stop here for a moment. Because that was double odd. One, because it's not long since we were in the wood and you were complaining about how wet it was. And two, because that is just about the first time that I have ever heard you have a good word to say about anything. So what's going on?"

"I'm just saying," said Henry.

"I got a pretty good idea." Thursday's head popped up out of the long grass. "Hey, Henry – do you hear a voice in your head?"

"Yes," said Henry. "I mean, no. Everything's nice and normal."

"It looks like your Malvalian cat has already got his operation up and running," said Thursday. "They always work the same way. It's a three-stage strategy – what we call the three Bs. Stage one – Imitate. Stage two – Hypnotize. Stage three – Steal."

"What do you mean, three Bs?" said Eddy. "There isn't a single B in any of those words."

"So it doesn't translate well," said Thursday. "But the strategy works. First the Malvalian arrives in a body that looks like a creature from the target planet. In this case, a cat. That's the Imitate. Then comes the Hypnotize. The Malvalian records a message on his communications interface, and his voice is transmitted straight into the brains of the local creatures. Everyone within range is completely taken over. Then the Malvalian gets them to do all the work that's needed – building, digging, blowing things up, whatever. They just do what they are told without question, and think everything is fine. That's what is happening in that town of yours."

"Has Henry been hypnotized?" said Eddy.

"Not yet, kid," said Thursday. "It takes a while for that to happen. But this is the really clever part. The Malvalian has to keep the whole plan secret from everyone who is just passing by. Anyone who only comes to visit the place, like that guy on the weird wheely thing we just saw going by, gets a message in their brain that it's a lovely day and everything is normal. They forget whatever they have seen going on, and if anyone asks, that's what they say – lovely and normal. That way, no one on the entire planet gets any idea that there's something wrong until stage three. Steal."

"And by then it's too late to stop them taking what they came for," said Eddy.

"Exactly," said Thursday. "Luckily the voice doesn't affect me." He tapped his head with one of his front legs.

"The thickest, shiniest skull in this quadrant of the galaxy. The beams just bounce off. But what beats me is why you two kids ain't getting it?"

"I don't know. I can't hear a voice at all. Wait a minute – I think I've got it," said Eddy. "It must be our hats. My auntie knitted them. I noticed before that Millie couldn't hear the cat's voice when she had hers on."

"Show me," said Thursday.

Eddy bent down so he could see the bobble hat.

"Aha!" said Thursday. "So, how come your auntie knows about signal disruption technology?"

"About what?"

"The shiny stuff," said Thursday. "With the little fronds that break down the signal and make it harmless. Stop you being hypnotized."

"It's tinsel," said Eddy. "We put it on trees at this time of year."

"What's the point of that?" said Thursday. "Who would try to hypnotize a tree?"

"Lovely day," said Henry. "Really normal."

"I need to get him away from here," said Thursday. "If he stays long enough for the voice to take control of him, all the tinsel in the world won't break the spell. I'd better not come into town anyway. If that Malvalian cat spots me, he'll know something's up. Me and Henry will meet you back at the podule. You do what you have to do – and good luck, kids."

It was then that they noticed the cats. Six of them, standing by the road sign, heads and tails held high and proud. Watching.

"Thursday," said Eddy, "those cats. It looks like they're checking us out. Could they be more Malvalians in disguise?"

"No. They only ever send one Malvalian down. It's all they ever need. But the cats round here could be under mind control as well. So watch out for them. And remember – keep your hats on, if you don't want to end up a mindless hypnotized slave."

"It's a lovely day," said Henry.

"Yeah, yeah," said Thursday. "Come on, pal. Let's get out of here so you can clear your head." He led Henry back in the direction of the podule.

Millie smiled at the cats that were standing by the road sign.

"Nice kitties," she said. "Can I stroke them?"

One by one, the cats drew back their lips and hissed, hackles raised.

"Not nice kitties," said Eddy.

The biggest of the cats, a black and white tom, looked like he was scowling at them. This was partly because the markings of the fur on his face gave him that expression, and partly because he was scowling at them.

"I don't think they want us to go past," said Eddy.

The black and white tom sat back, raised a front paw, and unsheathed a set of pearly white claws.

"Perhaps we need a password," said Millie.

"Cats don't even use ordinary words," said Eddy. "What sort of password could they have?"

"Mew?" said Millie.

"Hang on, though," said Eddy, "maybe there is something we could try."

He took a couple of paces towards the cats. The black and white tom flexed his claws threateningly.

"Lovely day," said Eddy. The tom's ears twitched. "And everything's normal."

The tom sheathed his claws. The cats moved aside, making room for Eddy and Millie to pass between them.

"So there was a password," said Millie. "I was right, wasn't I? Go on, say it! Say it!"

"You were right," Eddy admitted.

"Thank you, I'm sure," said Millie. "Lovely day!" And then her tummy gave a loud rumble. "I need something to eat," she said. "Right now."

"Okay," said Eddy. "We'll head to my house. There's bound to be some food. And we can pick up a few things while we're there."

He hoped he would be able to leave Millie with her parents, as well. It would be a lot easier to try to save the world without her in tow.

"Keep your eyes open on the way," he added.

"What are we looking for?"

"I don't know. Anything that isn't normal. And probably isn't lovely, either."

MUMMY

It was still the same Tidemark Bay. The same buildings. The same streets. The same noisy seagulls wheeling through the same salty air. But as Eddy and Millie walked through the town, it felt like something was lacking – like drinking a glass of orange made with too much water and not enough squash.

It was the people. No one quite looked them in the eye as they passed by. No one shouted or argued or complained. No one was flustered or frazzled or frantic. They all went about their business coolly, calmly and with barely a word. Even when a man stumbled over the kerb and dropped the crate of eggs that he was

140

carrying smack onto his foot, breaking lots of shells and probably a couple of toes to go with them, all he did was pick up what was left of his load and say "Lovely day!" as he hopped off on his way.

"It's like everyone is half asleep," said Eddy. *Or half dead,* he thought. But he didn't say that to Millie.

What Tidemark Bay didn't lack were cats. Dozens of them, everywhere they looked. Perched on top of postboxes, strutting across the roof of the bus shelter, sharpening their claws on tree trunks, yowling at each other from the tops of parked cars, and generally looking like they owned the town. And all of them eyeing Eddy and Millie as they made their way along the street.

"Will Mummy and Daddy be home?" said Millie, as they got near to Eddy's house.

"I hope so," said Eddy. He didn't tell her that he also hoped that her mum and dad wouldn't turn out to be as dizzy and dopey as everyone else in town. If they were hypnotized, he wouldn't be able to leave Millie with them, because he didn't know whether they would look after her. He didn't know whether they were going to give Millie the hugs and cuddles that she must be

expecting either, and he was worried that she would be upset about that – so worried that he barely had time to think about how he would feel if his own parents were the same.

BRRRP! said Millie's stomach as they walked up the front path. BRRRUUUPP!

"Are you alright?" said Eddy. "We need to keep an eye on you after you drank that Liquoid."

"I'm just hungry," said Millie. "And so is my tummy."

"Hello!" Eddy shouted, as he unlocked the front door. No answer.

"Food!" shouted Millie, pushing past him and making a dash for the kitchen.

"Why is the cupboard full of cat food?" he heard her calling seconds later. "There are stacks and stacks and stacks of tins and boxes of it."

"I've no idea," said Eddy, as he caught her up. She was right. There was nothing else in there at all. "Let's try the fridge."

That was more like it. There was some cooked chicken. Or rather, some cooked chickens. Six of them.

"You start on one of these," he said. "And I'll get some to take back for Henry and Thursday. They'll be hungry, too. I'll go and grab my backpack from under the stairs."

He had just found it when he heard the rattle of a key in the front door. His mum stepped into the hallway.

"What a lovely day," said his mum in a flat voice. "Nice and normal." She walked straight past him without a glance and headed towards the kitchen. *She's hypnotized just like the others*, Eddy thought. And now he didn't need to think how he would feel if his parents were the same as everyone else. He knew how he felt. Terrible.

His mum found Millie sitting at the kitchen table with a half-gnawed drumstick in each hand, and the rest of one of the chickens in front of her.

"You can't eat that," his mum said, grabbing the roasted bird. "It's not normal. Chicken is for the cats."

"Mine!" Millie shouted, dropping one of the drumsticks and grabbing the other side of the chicken. It came apart in their hands and fell to the floor in pieces.

Eddy's mum bent down to pick up the wrecked chicken. There was a knock at the door.

"The others must be here," his mum said, "just like they normally are." She went to let them in. "And leave that chicken for the lovely cats," she called.

"Quick," said Eddy. "She didn't say anything about the other five in the fridge. Let's get a couple of them into my backpack while she's not looking."

They just had time to stuff the birds inside and do up the zip before the rest of the family piled into the kitchen.

"Lovely day," said Eddy's dad.

"Lovely," agreed Aunt Maureen and Uncle Ken. Millie ran over to them, arms outstretched for a hug.

"Mummy," she shouted. "I missed you while I was in space. It was horrid."

"What are you talking about, dear?" Her mother brushed her away. "Space, indeed. Everything here has been perfectly normal."

"Daddy!" Millie turned to Uncle Ken. "Did you miss me?"

"Don't be silly, Millie," he answered. "We were only out for a couple of hours working on the project."

The project. Eddy's ears pricked up. He didn't know what the project was, but he reckoned it must be part of the Malvalian plan. If he and Millie waited here to follow their parents when they went out again, the grown-ups would probably lead them straight to whatever the alien had them working on.

"But we were gone for ages," said Millie. "It was horrible."

"Nonsense," said her dad. "It's a lovely day. Nothing horrible about it."

"Stop it!" shouted Millie, on the edge of tears. "I don't like it!"

"They're hypnotized, remember," Eddy said gently. "Like everyone round here."

Millie dashed out of the room. She was back almost immediately, clutching a long strand of silver tinsel that she had pulled from the Christmas tree. She climbed onto a chair and wrapped the tinsel round her father's head.

"Now stop being hypnotized and be you," she said. "Tell me a joke."

"No time for jokes," said her dad.

"But you always tell jokes," said Millie.

"I'm afraid that tinsel's not going to work," said Eddy. "Remember what Thursday said. Once someone's mind is being controlled, tinsel isn't enough to break the hold."

"Lovely hat, dear," said Aunt Maureen.

"Lovely sparkle," said Eddy's mum.

"Lovely," said Uncle Ken.

"Will they ever get right again?" asked Millie.

I don't know, Eddy thought.

"Of course they will," he said. "You wait and see."

One thing was clear, Eddy realized glumly. He was stuck with Millie. As if trying to save the world wasn't enough responsibility for one boy.

CHUNKY

"Everyone sit down for lunch," said Eddy's mum. She took three plates from a dresser, and set them at the head of the table, then put a whole chicken on the middle plate and divided the pieces of the bird that had fallen on the floor between the other two.

"I want some of the middle one, please," said Millie. But none of the grown-ups replied.

Eddy's dad handed round six forks, while his mother went to the cupboard and pulled out six cans of cat food.

"All grab one of these," she said.

"I'm not eating that," said Eddy.

"Don't be silly, dear," said his mother. "It's exactly what we normally have. Come on. Tuck in."

The grown-ups eagerly ripped the lids off the cans and plunged their forks in. Eddy's dad pulled out a pale brown lump and popped it in his mouth.

"Lovely chunks," he said as he chewed.

"And lovely jelly," agreed Eddy's mum.

Millie sat, arms folded, scowling at the can in front of her.

"Come on, Princess," said Uncle Ken. "You need to eat some lunch. Aren't you hungry?"

"I'm starving," said Millie. "But this isn't proper food. I'd rather eat sandworms, thank you."

"Don't be cheeky, Millie," said Uncle Ken. "It's delicious. Look." He stuffed a large forkful into his mouth and made exaggerated "yum yum" noises.

"Ewwwww!" said Millie.

"I'm not going to let you waste good food, young lady," said Uncle Ken. "If you're going to be so picky we'll have to do it like we did when you were tiny." He dipped a fork into Millie's can of cat food and pulled out a glistening pinkish piece. "Here comes the train," he said, pushing the fork slowly towards her mouth, "into the tunnel."

"No trains today," said Millie. "The tunnel is closed for the Christmas holidays." She clamped her lips tight.

"You're missing a real treat," said her mum. "It's lovely."

"Don't blame me if you are hungry later," said Uncle Ken.

A couple of mean-looking moggies suddenly jumped up onto the far end of the table near the plates of chicken. They both looked like they knew their way round a catfight. One had a half-chewed ear, and the other a scarred bald patch over one eye.

"Hey! Get down!" said Eddy, shooing them away. "You're not allowed in here."

"What are you doing, Eddy?" said his dad. "Of course they are allowed in here. We left the front door open for them. Don't listen to him," he said, turning to the cats. "You enjoy your lunch."

The cats stared at Eddy for a moment, their eyes narrow and hard, and then each chomped into one of the plates of chicken pieces.

"That's not fair," said Millie. "Why do they get chicken? I want chicken. That chicken." She pointed to the whole chicken on the middle plate.

"Don't be silly," said her mother. "You can't have that. That's for Ginger Tom."

As if his name was a signal, a ginger cat leaped onto the tabletop, landing next to his lunch. He skidded across the polished surface, and came to a halt in front of Eddy.

Eddy looked at Ginger Tom.

The trouble with cats, thought Eddy, *is that they are really hard to tell apart. Of course, they have different colours of fur, but once you get past that, a lot of them look very much alike.*

This one looked very much like Drax G'varglestarg.

Was it?

Back in the house where it had all started? Back with a couple of bruiser bodyguards and a plump roast chicken all to himself?

That made sense.

Ginger Tom, who of course really was the Malvalian Drax G'varglestarg in cat disguise, looked at Eddy and Millie. Funnily enough, Drax was thinking much the same thing as Eddy. That humans were really hard to tell apart, but these two looked very much like the pair that had been sent away in the podule. But they couldn't be – could they? Still, why worry? It would make no difference. As long as they were hypnotized like all the rest.

Drax stared at Eddy's untouched can of cat food.

"I think he's wondering why you aren't eating your lunch," said Eddy's mum.

Now Eddy was sure of it. Drax G'varglestarg. Mr Furrytummysnugglepaws. Ginger Tom. The Malvalian. A lot of names for just one cat.

This cat.

And if this cat realized that he and Millie weren't hypnotized, that they were spies plotting to stop the plan to steal all the water, what would Drax do to them? Eddy didn't want to think about it. Not with hundreds of cats stalking through the town, all of them with sharp teeth and claws, all of them controlled by the Malvalian.

The ginger cat padded back across the table, took a bite of chicken, and turned to watch Eddy.

There was only one thing to do. Eddy leaned across to Millie and whispered in her ear, "Can you do something really grown up for me?"

"Of course I can," said Millie. "I am nearly five."

"Good. I think that cat is *the* cat, and it is very, very important that it looks like we are hypnotized like everyone else, or we will be in big trouble. So we have to do what everyone else is doing. Which means that we are going to have to eat this cat food."

"Ewwww!" said Millie. "Spew!"

"We're each going to take a forkful, and I'm going to count to three, and then we are going to swallow it. Okay?"

"I will try," said Millie.

Eddy stuck his fork into the can and loaded it with cat food. He held it up. The jelly quivered on the prongs.

"One. Two. Three."

The jelly slithered on his tongue. He bit into a chunk. It was chewy and mildly meaty.

He swallowed it down as quickly as possible.

"Mmm!" he said. "Lovely!" And then "Mmm!" again, hoping that might just about make it sound as if he meant it.

"Ukkkk!" said Millie. "Ickkk! Urrghh!" Then after a few seconds, "Oh! It's not that bad. Better than worms." She took another forkful. "In fact, it's quite nice. And I am starving."

That turned out to be enough to convince Drax, who took a few more hurried bites of chicken, then disappeared out of the house again, with the two mean moggies trailing behind.

Eddy put his fork down next to his can of cat food. That was quite enough of that.

A few moments later, four forks clattered into four empty cans.

"Lovely," said four grown-up voices.

"Right," added Eddy's dad, rising out of his chair.

"Time to get back to the project."

"Come on," Eddy said to Millie, after their parents had left the room. "We need to go with them."

"Do we have to?" said Millie.

"Yes," said Eddy. "It's our chance to see what this project is. It must be what Ginger Tom – Drax – has got them all working on. And if we can get some photos of it, we'll be able to convince people outside that something is wrong here. So let's get moving."

"But I haven't finished my can yet," said Millie. She lifted out an enormous forkful of cat food and jammed it into her mouth.

PLLLRRRRRRP! said her stomach.

154

SHINY

Eddy and Millie found the four grown-ups putting their coats on in the hall.

"I'm taking this mirror," said Eddy's dad, lifting it down from the wall.

"Lovely," said Eddy's mum. "I've got all the pan lids and Maureen's going to carry the rolls of kitchen foil."

"And I've grabbed the silver tray from the sideboard," said Uncle Ken. "Hey, I wonder if this tinsel would be any good?" He unwound the strand that Millie had wrapped round his head.

"What are those things for?" Millie asked Eddy.

"I don't know," said Eddy. "But we're going to go with them and find out."

"I don't like people being hypnotized," said Millie. "I want them to be like they used to be."

"Me too," said Eddy. "That's why we need to persuade the government or the army or someone in charge that the cat is an alien. Then they will stop his plan to steal the water, and everything will go back to how it was before."

At least, I hope so, he thought. But he didn't say that to Millie. He was trying to hide how worried he was for her sake. But it wasn't easy.

Eddy pulled his backpack on, and he and Millie followed the four adults out of the house. Millie had grabbed her cuddly Horaceboris from where she had left him when she and Eddie had first gone to see the podule in the woods, along with a small bag that she had stuffed with comics and crayons and paper. She held Horaceboris by the hand as they joined a stream of people on the street, all carrying shiny metal objects, and all heading in the same direction, down towards the harbour.

"Stay close to me," said Eddy. "I'm going to ask people some questions to try and get clues about what this is all for."

It took just a few minutes for Eddy to gather two important pieces of information.

One – that it was a lovely day.

Two – that everything was normal.

Apart from that, no one said anything. They just kept walking.

Millie's stomach had plenty to say, however. It was making very odd noises – squelches and rumbles and raspberries.

"Are you feeling okay?" said Eddy.

"My tummy's a bit funny," said Millie. "But I think it is just wind."

The nearer they got to the harbour, the thicker the crowd became. By the time they reached the waterfront there was a wall of people in front of them, blocking their view.

"What is this?" said Millie.

"I don't know," said Eddy. "Let's just wait with everyone else and see what happens next."

What happened next was not much. And it turned out to be in no hurry to finish. But eventually they shuffled forward, the people in front of them moved away, and they had a clear view.

Ahead of Eddy lay the familiar shape of Tidemark Bay's harbour, a wide horseshoe of rock and stones.

What was not familiar was the lattice of scaffolding that towered around the harbour wall. Almost all the poles were bare, but at the far end was a patch that had been decked out with shining objects that glittered in the weak winter sun.

"What is it?" said Millie. "What are they making?"

"I've no idea," said Eddy. "But it's very odd. And anyone who saw this would know that something strange was going on. Let's take some photos and get out of here."

He pulled his phone out of his pocket, turned on its camera, and raised it for the first shot.

"MWWWAAAAAOW!"

A large cat jumped down from the harbour wall and landed in front of him, hissing and spitting. Four more emerged from the forest of people's legs, claws unsheathed and snarling.

"They don't like that, do they?" said Eddy. He slipped the phone back into his pocket. The cats stopped snarling but continued to eye him suspiciously.

"I can take the pictures," said Millie. "I can hold up

Horaceboris and hide the camera behind him. I will be a spy and no one will know because they will think I am just a sweet little girl."

"I don't know," said Eddy.

"I can be sweet," said Millie fiercely.

"What if you break it?"

"I do not break everything," said Millie. "And anyway it's not my fault. And anyway have you got a better idea?"

Eddy waited for a moment until the cats lost interest and wandered away, then slipped his phone to Millie. She tucked it behind her cuddly.

"Won't be long," she said.

"We should stick together," said Eddy.

But she had already disappeared into the crowd.

Eddy watched for her. All around him, shining metal objects caught the light as people carried them down to the harbour. What were they for? What was the cat planning to do? How did it fit with stealing the water? At least the photos would prove that something was wrong here. And then someone would have to believe him and take over the job of stopping it.

He was just beginning to wonder if something had happened to Millie when he heard her voice behind him.

"The rabbit will sleep in his burrow tonight."

"What rabbit?" said Eddy. "What are you talking about?"

"It's spy talk," said Millie.

"Just give me the phone back and we'll get out of here," said Eddy.

"Don't you know anything?" said Millie. "Spies don't talk to each other like that. I've seen it on TV. They do special code talking so that no one else can understand what they mean. You've got to do it too. You've got to do spy talk back to me or I won't play any more."

He didn't want to argue with her. They would just draw attention to themselves. And that was the last thing they needed.

"Alright," he sighed.

"Start again," said Millie. She skipped round in a wide circle and came up behind him. "The rabbit will sleep in his burrow tonight."

Eddy tried to think up a suitable answer.

"But the squirrel will sit watching his nuts," said Eddy. "Now can I have it?"

"No," said Millie.

"Why not?"

"Because that wasn't the right answer."

"Oh, come on," said Eddy loudly. A couple of the cats wandered over again and stared at them. "I don't like the way those cats are looking at us. We'd better get moving. You can give it back to me once we're out of town." He grabbed her hand and led her away from the harbour. "Lovely day," he called back towards the cats. "And everything's normal."

They found Henry and Thursday back by the podule. Thursday had scuttled halfway up a tree, and was hanging from a thick branch by most of his legs, and waving the others in the air.

"Just trying to dry them off," he called. "That wet ground is very bad for my feet."

Henry was sitting on a fallen tree trunk playing a slow tune on his armpit.

Eddy pulled off his backpack and reached inside.

"I brought you some chicken," he said.

"It's not my favourite," said Henry. "But I suppose it's better than nothing."

"I can tell your head is better," said Eddy. "You're not saying everything is lovely any more."

"What about my head?" said Henry, chewing on a

chicken leg. "I don't remember anything being wrong."

"So, kid," said Thursday, climbing down the tree trunk. "What's the news?"

"The town is in a mess," said Eddy. "Everyone's hypnotized. Drax is in charge – he's calling himself Ginger Tom. And he's got the real cats on his side. And they are building something in the harbour. I don't know what. But we got some photos."

"*I* got some photos," said Millie. She handed the phone back to Eddy. "See. I did not break it. And that will wipe off."

"What is it?" said Eddy.

"It smells like yoghurt. Strawberry, I think," said Millie.

"How on Earth did yoghurt get all over my phone?"

"I don't know," said Millie. "It's just a mystery."

Eddy rubbed the worst of it off on his coat sleeve and scanned through the photos.

"I was a very clever spy," said Millie. "I pretended I was just doing selfies."

"But these *are* just selfies," said Eddy. Millie leaned across to look at the screen.

"I look nice in that one, don't I?" she said.

"Never mind that," said Eddy, flicking through the pictures. "Ah, here's one. You can just see a bit of the harbour construction over your shoulder. Thursday?" Eddy held out the phone to him. "Do you know what this is?"

"Sure," said Thursday. "It's that primitive communication machine you were using earlier."

"No," said Eddy. "In the picture. Behind her shoulder."

"Beats me," said Thursday. "But it's something."

"I wonder if there are any better pictures," said Eddy. "Oh. It's stuck. The phone won't do anything."

"I did not break it," said Millie. "It was the yoghurt."

"Well at least we've got one picture that we can show," said Eddy. "And you can see that something weird is happening down at the harbour. There's a police station in the next town – Saltburn Sands. I think it's time to go down there and show them our evidence. They won't be able to ignore us now."

EMERGENCY

Sergeant Frank Constable loved the days before Christmas. He loved the fact that he could put a fir tree on the front desk in the Saltburn Sands police station, and decorate it with little flashing blue lights, and top it off with a fairy dressed in full police uniform and waving a magic truncheon.

He loved the way that everyone was so full of festive spirits that they forgot all about doing the sort of things that meant he had to arrest them. He loved how this gave him all the time he wanted to put his feet up and look through catalogues for garden sheds and decide which one he was going to treat himself to when he retired next summer.

In short, he loved the fact that it was so much quieter and calmer and lazier than the rest of the year.

Usually.

But not today.

Today, he had been getting cranky phone calls from people in Saltburn Sands all through his lunch break. Calls about noises in the woods that led down towards Tidemark Bay. Calls about a big shambling grey-blue figure seen through the trees – one said it was a yeti, one a big ape, and one a giant furry bathmat on legs. He knew that if he made the effort to go and have a look all he would find was someone out for a walk in a shaggy jumper. Or a big dog. These sorts of reports always turned out to be a big dog or a shaggy jumper. Except that one time when it was a big dog *in* a shaggy jumper.

And now, just as he was settling down to admire some very attractive sheds that looked like old railway carriages, the police station door rattled open and in strode a boy with a bulging backpack, a man in a tattered army uniform with most of a roast chicken in his hand, and a sweet little moppet in a pink princess dress carrying an ugly cuddly toy. Sergeant Constable feared the worst – this could mean that he was going to have to do something.

The moppet stomped up to the counter, and slapped something heavy and metallic down on it.

FLUMP! went her stomach.

"Ooh, pardon," said the moppet.

Sergeant Constable eyed the metal thing curiously. It appeared to be a door handle. A door handle very like the one on the front door of the police station.

"It did fall off," said the moppet.

Very like it indeed.

"Is that my door handle?" said Sergeant Constable.

"It might be," said the moppet. "If your door handle does need mending."

"I'll have to write a report on that," said Sergeant Constable.

"I did not break it," said the moppet. "But what would happen if somebody had?"

"Never mind that," said Eddy.

"It's no good saying never mind," said Sergeant Constable. "That's police property, that is."

"We need to talk about something much more important," said Eddy. "We're here to report an emergency."

"Oh, dear," said Sergeant Constable. "I was afraid that you might be. Go on then. If you must."

"He'll never believe you," said Henry, through a mouthful of chicken. "Not in a million years."

"We've been invaded," said Eddy.

"Who has?" said Sergeant Constable.

"Tidemark Bay. The world. We need to tell someone."

"I see," said Sergeant Constable. "Don't you think that if we were being invaded we'd have heard it on the news?"

"We are the news," said Eddy. "This is how news starts. Something happens, and someone reports it."

"Man!" said Millie. "Listen!"

"It's an alien," said Eddy. "We've been invaded by an alien from space."

"An alien," Sergeant Constable said slowly. "Ay. Lee. En," he repeated. Even more slowly.

"It probably sounds ridiculous," said Eddy.

"Well that's the first sensible thing you've said since you came in," said Sergeant Constable. "And you're not the first to report this. Take my word for it – it will just be a shaggy pullover. Or a big dog."

"What are you talking about?" said Eddy.

"I've been getting calls," said Sergeant Constable. "This alien you think you've seen. You're going to tell me that it's big and bluey-grey and wandering in the woods, aren't you?"

"No," said Eddy. "It's nothing like that. I mean, there *is* a big bluey-grey alien wandering in the woods, yes. It looks just like that cuddly toy that my cousin is carrying, only much much bigger. But that's not the one we need to worry about right now. The one we need to worry about is small and ginger and looks like a cat."

"Do you know that it is a serious offence to waste police time?" said Sergeant Constable.

"What can you see in this photo?" said Eddy, thrusting his phone towards the policeman.

"Her," said Sergeant Constable, pointing to Millie.

"Behind her," said Eddy.

"Nothing," said Sergeant Constable. "The screen's gone blank. I think your phone has died."

"Naughty yoghurt," said Millie.

"I told you he wouldn't believe you," said Henry. "And I was right."

"But it is true," said Millie. "There is a spaceship and trees that run away and robots and things that suck worms and it is not really a cat it is like a big orange octopus dressed in a cat body."

"You're starting to annoy me. Now run along and stop bothering me with this nonsense," said Sergeant Constable. "I don't know – first it's one alien, then it's two aliens…"

"And now it's three aliens," said Thursday, suddenly poking his head out of Eddy's backpack, where he had been hiding from view and keeping his feet dry. "And this alien thinks you need to start listening to what these guys are telling you."

"That policeman can move ever so fast for an old person, can't he?" said Millie.

The speed with which Sergeant Constable had reacted to Thursday's unexpected appearance was, indeed, impressive. As was the distance that he had covered in jumping on top of the filing cabinet. From a standing start.

"What," said Sergeant Constable in a quivering voice, pointing a quivering finger, "is that?"

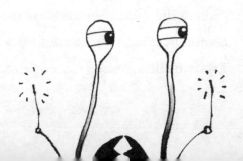

21
FUNNY

=Ha-ha!=
=Ha-ha!=
=Hee-hee!=
=A-ha-ha-haaa!=
=Ha-ha!=
=Hee-hee!=

"Yeah, yeah," said Thursday. "And I'm charmed to meet you, too."

"He's here to help," said Eddy. "To save the planet."

"And he's really an…um…" said Sergeant Constable from on top of the filing cabinet.

"Alien," said Eddy. "Yes, he is."

"See," said Millie. "I told you to listen."

"I don't get the – I mean it's not – just what is going on here?" said Sergeant Constable.

"At last," said Eddy. "We're getting through to you. So here is what is happening. We're being invaded. Everyone in Tidemark Bay has been hypnotized, and they are building something that must be part of the alien's plan to steal all the water. That's the cat alien's plan. Not this alien in my backpack. Or the bluey-grey alien in the woods. Are you with me so far?"

"Ummm," said Sergeant Constable. Which was pretty good considering how much he was trying to take in at once.

"We need to tell someone important about it so they can stop it before it's too late."

"I don't know," said Sergeant Constable. "I mean, I can't go ringing my Chief Inspector just like that to tell him there's a thing in your backpack and—"

"The name's Thursday Cornflake," said Thursday.

"That is not going to help," said Sergeant Constable. "I need to think what to do."

"Climbing down off the filing cabinet would be a good start," said Henry.

"Off the...? Oh, yes," said Sergeant Constable, slithering to the ground with a bump. "And then I'd better come down to Tidemark Bay and take a look with my own eyes. If I'm going to tell the Chief, I'll need to know what I'm talking about. I'll just get my notebook."

"If you're going to come down, you'll need this was well," said Eddy. He reached into his coat pocket and pulled out a long strand of silver tinsel. "Wind it round your hat – it will protect you from being hypnotized."

"Tinsel round my hat?" said Sergeant Constable. "But I'll look ridiculous. If anyone sees me they'll…ohh! Wait just one minute. I get it. I know what you are up to. As soon as I step outside that door looking like something that fell off a Christmas tree, one of your mates will be snapping away, and before you can say 'Guilty as charged' my picture will be all over the interweb and everyone will be laughing at me, won't they?"

"No," said Eddy. "What are you talking about?"

"This whole thing," said Sergeant Constable, "the phone calls about the creature in the woods, all that – it's just a wind-up, isn't it? Just to get a picture of me with a sparkly head."

"You've got to believe us," said Eddy.

"Very funny. You know, you nearly had me there. But the joke's over now. You're rumbled, sunshine.

Let it go," said Sergeant Constable. "Hang on. I know you, don't' I? You're the lad from the pet fancy-dress place. Me and the wife were down there a couple of weeks ago buying a Hero Hound outfit for her sister's poodle. Oh, yes, now I've got it – that thing in your backpack – it's just some dog in one of your hideous Halloween costumes, isn't it? How do you do the voice then? Ventriloquism, is it?"

"What is this clown gabbling on about?" said Thursday.

"I have to admit, you're very good," said Sergeant Constable. "When you said that, I couldn't see your lips moving at all."

"It's all real," said Eddy.

"You've given me a right good laugh," said Sergeant Constable. "Really livened up the day. But you'd better run along now."

"No. They are going to destroy the Earth."

"That's N – O – W…now," said Sergeant Constable. "Because I've got a load of paperwork to get through." He eyed the pile of shed brochures. "Unless you want me to round off the joke by locking you up."

"I was right, after all," said Henry.

174

"You're making a terrible mistake," said Eddy.

"Happy Christmas!" said Sergeant Constable. "Shut the door on your way out, would you?"

"I can't shut it," said Millie. "I told you – it did break."

They stomped outside. The light was beginning to fade as the early winter evening closed in. The day was getting gloomy. And so was Eddy.

"What are we going to do now," he said, "if no one is going to believe us and no one is going to help?"

"I guess there's always the Galactic Conservation Council," said Thursday. "If you can show them that this planet is something special, they have the power to order the Malvalians to stop what they are doing."

"What is costivation?" said Millie.

"It means keeping things as they are," said Eddy. "Not spoiling them. Nature and animals and stuff. We learn about it at school. Why didn't you tell us about this council before?"

"You only go to the Galactic Conservation Council when you have run out of other ideas," said Thursday. "They don't like coming out on planet inspections. They think they are even more important than they are

– which is kind of hard to imagine. And they are very, very hard to convince. Most planets don't even come close. And if you fail, it's over. No second chances. It's going to be difficult."

"Right now I'll take difficult," said Eddy. "As long as it gives us a chance."

"Then I'll put in a call," said Thursday. He waggled his antennae. "If I can get a signal on this planet. Hold on."

He scuttled up the side of the police station. "That's better," he said. "The message to the Council is on its way."

"So what do we do now?" said Eddy.

"We wait for them to call back," said Thursday. "It could take a while. Especially if they are having dinner."

22

CHOOSY

It did take a long time for the Galactic Conservation Council to call back. They still hadn't done it by nightfall. Eddy, Millie, Henry and Thursday finished what was left of the chickens for supper. Eddy didn't want to risk going home to sleep, because he was worried that if he rolled over in bed and his bobble hat came off, by morning he would be hypnotized just like his parents. So they all bedded down in the podule. Except for Thursday, who bedded up, hanging from the ceiling.

Eddy couldn't sleep. His head was full of worries. And the noises didn't help. Henry was snoring steadily, and Millie's tummy kept rumbling and grumbling and making strange whistling noises so loudly that he was surprised it didn't wake her up. He hoped that this wasn't a sign that the Liquoid professor that she had glugged down was going to make her ill.

When sleep finally came to Eddy, it brought weird dreams.

A ginger cat was sitting on the edge of the harbour in Tidemark Bay, sucking up the water through a long drinking straw. With every suck the water level dropped, and the cat got fatter and rounder. Eddy tried to reach round it and grab the straw, but the monster cat kept growing extra paws that pushed him away, prodding at his ribs and—

"Wake up!"

– digging into his chest and –

"Come on kid, wake up!"

– and poking him in the stomach –

"We've got to get moving!"

– and his eyes were open and Thursday was standing beside him and nudging him and saying, "I got the call back from the Council. It's time to get to work."

"Here's what happens now," said Thursday a few moments later, when Millie and Henry had joined him and Eddy outside the podule. "To save the planet you have to choose three things to show to the Galactic Conservation Council to prove that the place is special."

"Just three?" said Eddy.

"Just three," said Thursday. "They don't give you long to impress them."

"But there's so much planet," said Eddy. "How do we choose?"

"Quickly would be good," said Thursday. "The Council will be here this afternoon. You got just over five hours. And I got to warn you, the galaxy is a pretty spectacular place. I've seen things you tubies wouldn't believe. Giant crystal mountains that cast rainbows across the whole sky. Plants that chime like bells when the breeze blows. Make sure you choose something very special."

"I don't know where to start," said Eddy. "The Amazon rainforest? The pyramids? The Eiffel Tower?"

"I have no idea what those are," said Thursday. "But if you like them, fine. Just make sure you bring them here in time."

"We have to bring them here? Well then they are no good," said Eddy. "We'll have to pick something else. What about – oh, I don't know."

"Three things is one each," said Henry. "And I choose – pie."

"Pie?" said Eddy.

"Meat and potato," said Henry. "The greatest of all the pies. And let me tell you, if there's one thing I found out during my years in that zoo, it's that aliens can't cook. So if you want to impress them, I reckon a really good pie is the thing to do it."

"I've got one," said Millie. "A ephelant."

"An elephant?" said Eddy.

"That's what I said," said Millie. "It is very special and it has a trunk. So I choose it."

"Where do you think we are going to find an elephant?" said Eddy.

"At the zoo in Saltburn Sands," said Millie. "They have one. I have seen it."

"And how are we going to get it out?"

"I don't know," said Millie. "I am four and three-quarters, not a famous ephelant thief."

"We'd never get away with it. It's much too big."

"Then obviously you must make it smaller," said a deep voice. A strange voice, that seemed to come out of nowhere.

"Who said that?" said Eddy.

"It was my tummy," said Millie. "I think there is someone in there."

"My name is Blubblubblabblubblubblubblap," said Millie's tummy.

"The Liquoid professor?" said Eddy. "You mean you are still alive?"

"The oceans of my home world are raging pools of acid. If I can survive in them I can certainly survive in here. Though this is a lot smellier."

"But how can you talk to us?" said Eddy.

"I can flow through this whole body. A few moments

181

inside the brain were quite enough to learn your simple language," said the Professor. "It took a lot longer to practise how to vibrate in here to produce the required sounds."

"It's making my tummy wobble," said Millie.

"I have been listening to what you have been saying about the Malvalian plan to steal the water," the Professor went on. "I am going to help you stop them. We liquids must stick together, after all. I have one of the most brilliant scientific minds in the entire galaxy. And it sounds like you need me if you don't even know how to shrink things."

"Round here things generally stay the same size," said Eddy.

"How very dull," said the Professor. "And inconvenient. If you can't make things smaller, what do you do when you need to pack to go on holiday? Or get the family together to enjoy a game of Where Have I Hidden Grandma? You really mean you haven't invented a shrinking device?"

"My mum uses the washing machine," said Millie.

"If it will help you to beat the Malvalians," said the Professor from Millie's tummy, "I will build you one. We can use the technology from one of the engines on this podule."

"You know about the engines?" said Eddy.

"I should do," said the Professor. "The Malvalians forced me to design them."

"How do they go so fast?" said Eddy. "I thought that nothing could travel faster than light."

"You can't really be blamed for making mistakes like that," said the Professor. "Not with a brain like yours. Let me see if I can explain it in a way that even you can understand. To put it very simply, the engine shrinks a tiny strip of space in front of it, so that it has less far to go. And then it makes the space just behind itself a bit bigger, so it has already gone there. It fiddles around with the way time is passing, too. Do those things several million times a second, and you have a quantum wave accelerator engine that can zip along much faster than light."

"And I've got two of them," said the podule. "Eat my space dust!"

"And we can use one of them to make a shrinking machine that you can carry round," said the Professor.

"It sounds brilliant," said Eddy. "Will it take long to make?"

"Just a few minutes. It's not a difficult job. It's only rocket science, after all," said the Professor. "A child could do it. In fact, a child will do it. Millie's body simply has to follow my instructions. But we'll need something to put it in. A small case of some sort. I must flow back into contact with her brain so I can control what we are doing."

"You could use my phone," said Eddy. "It hasn't recovered from meeting that yoghurt. Will that do?"

It did. With the Professor directing her movements, Millie's little hands worked at tremendous speed, delicately fitting tiny electronic parts into the shell of Eddy's phone.

"It feels really funny," Millie said, as her fingers flashed and flitted at her task, "because I can't do this."

But it was soon done. Millie was now holding a totally refitted and amazingly advanced device.

With the job over, the Professor flowed down out of her brain.

"I've got my fingers back," said Millie. And dropped the phone.

Eddy dived forward and caught it just before it hit the ground.

"Oops!" said Millie. "But I did not break it."

"Not quite," said Eddy.

"But it was a good try," said Henry.

"And now to show you how it works," said the Professor, who was back in Millie's stomach. "Turn it on. I have connected the circuits inside so that all you do is point the camera at your target and click."

Eddy lined up a fallen tree trunk and pressed the button. For a couple of seconds the tree trunk glowed with a pale green halo. Then it suddenly shrank down to the size of a twig.

"Wow," said Eddy. "That's incredible." He picked up the tiny tree. "It has lost weight, too."

"That's all part of the effect. I've set the device so it will shrink things down to a size that you can fit in your pocket," said the Professor. "Now dial 3-2-1 and see what happens."

Eddy punched in the numbers.

"Nothing," he said. "I can't see anything different."

"Look around," said the Professor.

Eddy did. He spotted a bird that was flying between the bare branches of a nearby tree. Except that it looked more like it was fighting its way through glue. He could see every beat of its wings as if it was in a film running in super-slow motion.

"Has everything around us slowed down?" he asked.

"Strictly speaking, you have speeded up. As well as shrinking things, your device can interfere with the way that time flows through the space around it. I won't even try to explain this one. It involves using long complicated words that are so full of very advanced science that just hearing them could damage your brains. All you need to know is that one burst from your device gives you about ten minutes, while everyone on the outside only experiences thirty seconds. Now you had better turn it off to save the battery. Put that tiny tree down and stand well back because – well, you will see why."

Eddy hit the off button. As the power shut down, the tree trunk immediately returned to full size. The bird zipped past and up into the sky.

"Once it stops transmitting, the effects are cancelled instantly," said the Professor. "Just make sure you remember that."

"I will," said Eddy. "Don't worry."

"Let's go and get a ephelant!" said Millie.

23

BEAKY

"The shrinking device is great," said Eddy, "but we've got less than five hours to get our three things to show to the Galactic Conservation Council. So we need to move fast. We'll start with the pie. Then the elephant. And by then I should have decided what I'm going to choose. I just can't make up my mind."

Eddy, Millie and Henry were walking into the centre of Saltburn Sands. Thursday had stayed behind at the podule, partly to make sure that everything was ready for the arrival of the Council, and partly because they had all agreed that the job of collecting the things they needed wouldn't be made easier if the inhabitants of

Saltburn Sands caught sight of a giant cockroachy prawny creature from outer space and started running round the town screaming their heads off.

"Look. There's a supermarket over the road," said Eddy. "We can buy a pie in there."

"Buy? We're not going to buy it," said Henry. "I'm going to make it. These fingers are itching to get back in the baking game. The feel of raw pastry under your nails – you can't beat it. I shall make the finest pie that you have ever seen, from crust to gravy. All those years locked in the alien cage I used to wonder, why me? Now I know. I was born for this moment – to bake the pie that saves the world."

"But we haven't got anything to cook it in," said Eddy.

"I was an army cook, remember?" said Henry. "You don't get to be an army cook without learning how to knock up a field oven. A big cardboard box, a lot of silver foil to wrap it, a hole in the ground and a wood fire. It will be as good as any kitchen. You'll see."

"If you are sure," said Eddy.

"Never surer," said Henry.

"I've got all the money I saved to buy Christmas presents in here." Eddy pulled his wallet from his pocket.

"So let's shop."

It went pretty well. They soon found everything that Henry needed for his pies, and even remembered to buy something for breakfast. They stood on the pavement outside the shop, full of success and chocolate muffins.

"We came," said Eddy. "We shopped. We got the full list. Henry, you need to go back to the podule and build your field oven and bake pie as if the whole world is depending on you. Because it is."

But then Eddy and Millie had the job of stealing the elephant. And that was…well, it was like this.

Down at the Saltburn Sands Ocean Park and Zoo, the grey sky had started to drizzle. The animals were huddling miserably in their cages. Except the fish, obviously, who couldn't have cared less about the weather because they were already soaked to the gills. A gaggle of penguins stood hunched by their pool waiting hopefully for herrings. A pair of monkeys crouched in the next enclosure, baring their teeth and chattering. A handful of keepers sat on a damp bench under a canopy that didn't quite shut out the weather, sharing a flask of hot tea.

"There's the ephelant," said Millie, pointing to a large grassy enclosure opposite the monkey cage. "Let's use the shrinker and grab him."

"We can't just grab him," said Eddy. "There's a great big metal fence around his enclosure. We have to get past that to reach him."

"Shrink that too, then," said Millie.

"Not possible," the Professor's voice rumbled from her stomach. "The shrinking device doesn't have enough power stored to shrink everything in sight."

"Will you please shrink something soon?" said Millie. "I want to see it work again."

"There's a gate in the fence over there," said Eddy. "With a big padlock on it. What we need is one of the keepers."

"Are we going to shrink him?" said Millie.

"No. We need to get him to open the lock."

"I will do it," said Millie.

The keepers never stood a chance.

"Hello, men!" said Millie, advancing on them behind her brightest smile, and clutching Horaceboris.

"Hello, little girl," grunted the keepers.

"I do like your ephelant," said Millie. "What does it eat?"

"All sorts," said one of the keepers. "Hay. Carrots. Bits of wood."

"I don't think it eats wood," said Millie. "I think you are teasing me because I am four and three-quarters."

"Really," said the keeper.

"Show me," said Millie.

"Not now," said the keeper. "You'll have to wait till feeding time."

"Is it feeding time now?"

"No," said the keeper, looking at his watch. "In about an hour."

"How many carrots does he eat?"

"Loads. A whole sackful."

"How many is that? Forty-three? Two hundred and six? A million?"

"I don't know."

"Oh," said Millie. "Is it feeding time now?"

"No," said the keeper. "I said in about an hour."

"Is it a hour yet?"

"No," said the keeper.

"Is it nearly a hour?

"No."

"When will it be an—"

"For goodness' sake, Beaky," said one of the other keepers, "go and feed the elephant. It won't matter if we're early for once."

The keeper rose stiffly from his bench and walked towards the elephant enclosure. Millie trotted alongside him. Eddy followed them.

"Why do they call you Beaky?" asked Millie.

"More than twenty years I worked here," said the keeper, "and never a mistake. And then one day, I let a penguin escape. Slipped away from the Ocean Park while my back was turned during a rehearsal of Fishy Frolics. And would that lot let me forget it? Would they flip. Since then not one of them has called me by my proper name. It's Beaky, this and Beaky that."

They reached the elephant's enclosure. The elephant had seen them coming, and wandered over to the gate to see what was happening. The keeper picked a key from the large bunch attached to his belt, and turned it in the padlock. Then he pushed the gate open, his back towards Eddy and Millie.

"Stay there, you two," he said. "You're not allowed inside."

3-2-1 Eddy dialled on the shrinking device. Everything around them went into slow motion. He darted past the keeper, selected the camera on his phone, pointed it at the elephant and pressed. The animal glowed with a pale green halo for a second, and then – zzzzzzipppp.

"Yaaayyyy!" shouted Millie. She laughed delightedly.

"What is that extraordinary noise?" said the Professor. "It's like an earthquake in here."

"I'm laughing," said Millie. "Because it shrinked."

"Laughing," said the Professor. "I've never heard of that. Is it painful?"

"You're silly," said Millie. And laughed again.

It took Eddy a moment to spot the tiny elephant, which was hidden behind a dandelion. He reached into his pocket and pulled out an empty snackpack of raisins that he had left in there. He gently popped the animal inside the cardboard box, closed the lid, and put it back in his pocket, taking care to keep it the right way up.

"Let's go," he said to Millie. "We need to get well away from here before time gets back to normal again."

Millie paused for a moment to speak to the zookeeper. His back was still turned towards her, and he was moving as slowly as if he was wading through treacle.

"Thank you for the ephelant. And I don't think you will have to worry about them calling you Beaky any more. Bye bye, Trunky."

And she skipped after her cousin.

24

ARTY

"I don't know," said Eddy. "There are so many things to choose from and it's so important to get it right."

They were back in the centre of Saltburn Sands. The shrunken elephant was safely tucked inside the empty raisin packet in Eddy's pocket. But he still couldn't decide what he should choose to prove to the Galactic Conservation Council that Earth was special and had to be saved.

"Well get a move on," said Millie.

"I think it should be something that humans are really good at," said Eddy. "Maybe there's something here that will give me an idea."

They were standing in front of a large noticeboard, which was covered with posters advertising what was happening in Saltburn Sands.

"Like that," said Eddy, pointing at the board. "Look at all the things that are going on. The choir singing. A play. An exhibition of flower arranging. Grown-ups are always banging on about films and books and art and music and how great they are. We can show the Council one of those."

"Let's do music," said Millie. "I can play my recorder. We all learned a tune at school last term called Blue Cs. It goes like this: Toot-toot-toot –" she began to sing – "toot-toot-toot. Toooooot-toooooot-tooooooooooooooooot. Toot-toot-toot…"

"All on one note?" said Eddy.

"Yes. C," said Millie. "We are going to learn another note next term."

"I thought you were trying to save the planet," said the Professor. "Anyone who had to listen to that would want to destroy it."

"Rubbish," said Millie. "We did it at school and it made all the mummies and daddies smile. And some of them laughed out loud. One did it so much he fell off his chair."

"Maybe a painting would be better," said Eddy. "Hang on, what's this?"

In front of Eddy was a large poster which read:

OPEN STUDIO

TODAY ONLY – AN OPPORTUNITY TO APPRECIATE THE LATEST PAINTINGS BY INTERNATIONALLY FAMOUS ARTIST

MAXTON BANDERFIELD

FIRST LEFT. • TEA AND CAKES NOT SERVED.

"That," said Eddy, "sounds very promising."

The famous artist's studio was a vast loft with huge windows looking out over the broad sea. A few people were peering at paintings, large and small, that were hung on the other three walls. Next to an easel with an unfinished canvas on it stood a tall man with a small pointed beard on his chin and a paint-spattered suit on the rest of him. He was talking to a young woman who was recording his words on her phone.

"…feeling," he was saying, "I think that's what made me such a success as an artist. And, of course, my simply enormous talent. Don't forget to mention that to the readers of your newspaper."

Eddy looked round the room. He was surrounded by images of crashing waves and flying foam. The work of an internationally famous artist. One of these would surely do. But which one?

"Man!" Millie called as she strode up to the figure in the suit. "Did you do them?"

"Ah, the young. I always say one must encourage the young." He smiled. "All my work, yes – and don't touch that. Or anything."

"Have you got any with ponies on them?" said Millie.

"I paint the sea, child, the sea in all its moods and mystery," said Banderfield. "Not ponies."

"They could be having a swim," said Millie. "They can swim, you know. And that way you don't have to do their legs. They are the hardest part, I think. Is that why you paint the sea, because you can't do legs?"

"Amusing child," said Banderfield, "run along now, why don't you?"

"No thanks," said Millie.

"Which do you think is your best painting?" Eddy asked.

"I always say that my best painting is my next one," said Banderfield. "You should put that in your article as well," he told the reporter.

Millie looked at the half-empty canvas on the easel.

"Can you hurry up and finish it, please?" she said. "We need it today. Otherwise the space cat is going to take all the water and then you will be sorry because there won't be any sea left so you will have to paint something else and learn how to do legs right. So can we borrow it when you've done it?"

"Childhood imagination," Banderfield told the reporter. "Such a precious gift." He bent down and spoke quietly in Millie's ear. "No, of course you can't. Go away and stop annoying me." He turned his back and led the young woman towards the windows.

"That one will do," said Eddy. "Nice colours. I hope the Galactic Conservation Council like it." He took one of the smaller paintings down from the wall and tucked it under his coat. "I'll just adjust time so we can get away easily." He reached into his pocket with his free hand and pulled out the shrinking device.

"It's my go," said Millie. "I want to do it!"

Heads turned to see what the little girl was shouting about.

"Shh!" said Eddy. "We don't want them to spot what we are doing."

"Then give it to me!" said Millie. She snatched the device. Her fingers jabbed down on the number buttons as she did it.

1-2-3.

"That's the wrong way round," said Eddy.

"Oh dear," said Professor Blubblubblabblubblubblubblap.

"Press 3-2-1," said Eddy.

"I am," said Millie.

"I think we have a problem," said the Professor.

"It's not working," said Millie.

But it was.

"Run!" said Eddy.

Unfortunately for them, it was working in the wrong way. Eddy grabbed Millie's hand and almost dragged her off her feet as he ran as fast as he could towards the door.

But everyone else in the room was moving faster. Much faster. Walking towards him like they were in a crazy speeded-up film.

"What's happening?" said Eddy.

"Putting in the numbers the wrong way round makes the device work in reverse," said the Professor. "It has shifted time in the wrong direction."

Eddy felt hands grabbing for him. By the time he tried to wriggle away they already had a firm grip. Voices jabbered at him like angry gerbils. Someone was squeaking into a phone.

"How long will this last?" asked Eddy.

"For us about thirty seconds," said the Professor. "But everyone else will experience ten minutes."

The seconds whizzed by in a flurry of action. They were lifted up, feet off the ground, marched out of the building in a blur. For Eddy and Millie the world was running at an incredible speed. And it didn't return to normal until they were in the back of the police car.

CHEEKY

"Exhibit A," said Sergeant Constable. "An original Banderfield." He plonked the painting down next to his little Christmas tree on the front desk at Saltburn Sands police station. "Well?"

"We only needed to borrow it," said Eddy. "We were going to bring it back."

He wondered whether to try the shrinking device again. To alter time – the right way – and make a run for it. But when he felt in his pocket the device wasn't there.

"The law calls that stealing, young man," said the Sergeant. "Do you realize what a serious situation you are in?"

"We do," said Eddy, trying to calm things down.

He knew they had to get out of there fast, and if they were very polite and extremely sorry, maybe they could. Millie had got the idea as well.

"We were only playing," she said, "and as you are such a nice and kind and clever policeman, please let us go."

"Well—" Sergeant Constable began.

"What are you talking about?" said the Professor from Millie's stomach. "He's clearly a blundering idiot who has no idea what is happening round here."

"What was that?" said Sergeant Constable.

"Don't listen," said Eddy. "She just drank something that disagrees with her."

"Are you trying to be funny?" said Sergeant Constable. "That voice I heard. It was you doing your ventriloquism again, wasn't it? I've got two pieces of advice for you, sonny. Number one – that voice you did was completely wrong for a little girl. Far too deep. And number two, if you are trying to get locked up you are going the right way about it, so no more of your cheek. Understood?"

"Completely," said Eddy. He looked at the clock on the wall. They were due to meet the Galactic Conservation Council in just over an hour. Getting locked up would be a disaster. "We all understand that, don't we?" he added.

"Yes," said Millie. "I do. And so does Horaceboris." She clutched her cuddly tightly. Her tummy rumbled quietly.

"Let's have a look at the contents of your pockets then," said Sergeant Constable. He held up a clear plastic bag. Eddy could see coins, bits of string, shining tinsel, the raisin box with the elephant hidden inside it, and the shrinking device housed in his broken phone. The Sergeant must have been through their pockets after he'd bundled them into the car. Eddy hadn't noticed – but then everything had been a blur. "We'll see," the Sergeant went on, "if there's anything else here that you shouldn't have borrowed without asking."

The Sergeant tipped the contents of the plastic bag out onto the desk.

"Be careful with that raisin box," Eddy said.

"Why?" said the Sergeant. "What have you got in there?"

"Errrr…" Eddy bit his tongue. He could imagine how cheeky the real answer would sound.

He didn't have to imagine for long.

"It's a ephelant," said Millie.

"Right," said the Sergeant. "I warned you about giving me cheek. I was just going to ring your parents and let you off with a stiff word. But as you obviously think this is all a big joke, we'll see how funny you find a couple of hours in the cells."

"Please let us go," said Eddy. "We're very sorry, really we are. And we haven't got a couple of hours."

"I'll be the judge of that," said the Sergeant. "And I'd better turn this phone off. You won't be needing it in there."

"Don't!" shouted the Professor from Millie's tummy.

"Please listen," said Eddy. "That would be a really, really bad thing to do. If you turn it off, it will stop working."

"That is the general idea," said Sergeant Constable. He pressed the power button. The device blinked off. For a second everything was still. But then…

The elephant returned to its normal size. Very, very quickly.

When the force of a rapidly expanding elephant meets the resistance of a small cardboard box, ninety-nine times out of a hundred there is only going to be one result. And the other time as well.

The box exploded into a gazillion pieces.

The elephant continued to spread outwards and upwards, taking most of the ceiling with it. Broken ceiling tiles clattered to the floor.

The desk was next to go. It gave up its struggle with the huge weight that suddenly pressed down on it, and collapsed into a mess of shattered wood and plastic. The elephant's feet hit the floor with a bump as the painting, the shrinking device, the Christmas tree and everything else that had been on top of the desk went flying across the room.

The Sergeant's mouth fell silently open. It was hard to say who was more surprised by what had just happened – him, or the elephant.

The elephant had had enough of being trapped. First it had been stuck inside a cardboard box, and now it was squeezed into a very snug police station. And it wanted out. It started to turn round, to see which way to go. Being in the same small space as an elephant is not a good idea.

Unless you also happen to be an elephant, you will find that there is a lot of it, and not very much of you. And that is dangerous. Very dangerous indeed.

As the elephant turned to look for a way out, it stepped backwards.

Eddy realized with horror that its enormous right foot was about to come down on top of Banderfield's painting and the shrinking device, which had landed together on the floor. And its enormous left leg was heading for Millie, about to squash her against the wall.

He had to move. Fast. One side or the other. To rescue the painting that might save the world, or to get his cousin out of the way before she was turned into a very messy wall covering.

He jumped. For Millie.

Grabbing the sleeve of her pink princess dress, he hauled her out of the way as the elephant's massive haunch crunched into the police station brickwork. The noise almost drowned out the sound of the elephant's right foot trampling the shrinking device into tiny pieces and crunching down onto the painting.

The elephant spotted the entrance to the police station and headed out, converting the front door into a front very-large-hole-in-the-wall as it passed through.

Sergeant Constable finally spoke.

"What?" he said. Which summed things up pretty well.

"I told you," said Millie. "But oh no, you just wouldn't believe me."

"We hadn't even had that front door mended since last time you were here," Sergeant Constable mumbled. He wondered how he was going to explain all this to the Chief Inspector. He had a feeling that his retirement was going to come much sooner than he had been planning.

"We'll get off now, then," said Eddy.

"Duh!" said Sergeant Constable in a daze.

"We're in a bit of a hurry," said Eddy. "Bye!"

He led Millie out through the front very-large-hole-in-the-wall. It was a mess. And so were their plans. He had no elephant. No painting. Almost no time before the Galactic Conservation Council arrived. And absolutely no idea at all how to be ready for them.

"Agent Ginger Tom reporting to Malvalian Grand Control. Construction almost completed. Send pillaging fleet now. Report ends."

That is all they need to know, thought Drax. *No need to complicate things. And no need to make the effort to say more.* What he had found out couldn't possibly matter at this stage, even though it was extraordinary. It was something one of the tubeoids had said. Apparently, many of the information transmissions – "TV programmes" was their name for them – were not true. They were just made up. Including the ones about superpowered beings. Beetleman with his impenetrable body armour and razor-sharp pincers. Hero Hound and his amazing special abilities. The Weather Women who came on screen to tell the world where they were sending wind and rain and sunshine and snow that day. None of them could really do any of the fantastic things that they appeared to. There were as fake as his own disguise as Ginger Tom. If Grand Control knew that, they would have to rewrite half the mission databank. And they wouldn't like that. So he would keep it to himself.

Ginger Tom. He was getting to quite like that name. It had a bit of a swagger to it. A name that commanded respect from the cat guards.

He was starting to think that he had perhaps been a bit quick to write off the cats. Some of their activities were really very interesting. Especially the ones that involved small furry things that ran away when they were chased, or small feathery things that flew away. He wanted to find out a lot more about these small things. But he had never managed to get near enough to them. Not yet, anyway. Still, there was always next time.

But right now he fancied a bit of a sleep. That was another good idea that the cats had. Regular rests through the day. He stretched out and yawned. He had noticed that he had started making a strange noise when he relaxed. Purring, the tubeoids called it. Just like the real cats. He would have to think about that. When he woke up.

CLOUDY

"This is a disaster," said Eddy.

He and Millie had returned to the podule to find Henry sitting glumly in front of the smoking remains of a burned-out cardboard box wrapped in scorched strips of kitchen foil. His face and beard were smeared with soot. Around him lay his batch of unfortunate pies.

"It turns out that I'm a bit out of practice," said Henry. "I had a few difficulties with the pastry. And the filling. And my field oven caught fire. Until the rain put it out. I think that's why they are a bit overdone in places. And a bit underdone in others."

Eddy picked up one of the pies. On one side the pastry was hard and charred black, while on the other side it was pale and almost raw. And the whole thing was so flat that it looked like a Fluffy Wuffy Cushion Bunny had sat on it.

"I'm sure I'll do better next time," said Henry.

"You ain't got a next time," said Thursday, who was watching from a nearby tree. "The Galactic Conservation Council are due here any minute."

"Maybe this one's not so bad," said Henry, holding up one of his crusty victims. "It looks a bit less like a baked cowpat than the others." The pie fell to pieces in his hand, leaving a trail of thick brown gravy.

"It's not just the pies," said Eddy. "It's everything. No elephant. No painting. And no time to think of anything else while we were in Saltburn Sands. We were in such a hurry to get back here."

"I hate to tell you this, kid," said Thursday, "but right now your chances with the Council aren't looking great."

"Maybe there's something out here that we could show them," said Eddy. He looked round at the woods. The grey sky. The bare winter trees. The fallen leaves and soggy twigs on the ground. "Oh, I don't know. Maybe they'll just like the look of the place."

"We'll soon find out," said Thursday. "Here they come."

A puff of purple smoke curled out of nowhere. It spread and grew until it formed a ball of coloured cloud that was as tall as Eddy. Tiny bolts of lightning crackled through it.

"Is this it?" said a plummy voice from the purple cloud.

"Oh dear," said another. "Bit of a dump, isn't it?"

"It's the middle of winter," said Eddy. "You should see it in the summer – green leaves, blue sky, it's really beautiful."

"Who addresses the Galactic Conservation Council?" said the first voice.

"Me," said Eddy. "Eddy Stone. I'm here to save the Earth."

"Well you haven't made a very good start," said the first voice. "Not good at all."

"We're used to better than this," said the second voice. "If someone is trying to impress us."

"It's not that one is big-headed," said a third voice, "but when all the most advanced species in the galaxy have asked one to judge whether planets should live or die, and when one can harness the natural forces of the universe to punish anyone who would dare to disagree, like this..."

A crackle of lightning shot out of the purple cloud and instantly reduced a nearby tree to a small pile of smouldering ashes.

"…is it too much to expect a little fuss to be made of one? A red carpet? Some welcoming music? I don't think so."

"I could do 'Blue Cs'," said Millie.

"Please don't," said Eddy.

"I was hoping for drinks and nibbles," said the second voice.

"I must apologize, your high and mightinesses," said Thursday. "These are simple tubeoids who don't really understand how to behave in the presence of greatness like yourselves."

"Yes, yes – just show us the three things that you think prove this planet is worth saving, will you?" said the first voice.

215

"And don't take too long about it," said the second. "We've got a very important dinner party to get back to."

"Too long?" said Eddy. "We're talking about the fate of a whole planet here, and you hope it's not going to make you late for dinner?"

"Once again, I apologize to your honourable councillorshipnesses," said Thursday, scuttling in front of Eddy. "He doesn't mean—"

"Blah blah," interrupted the first voice. "Stop wasting time. What have you got for us?"

"I've got pie," said Henry. He pushed the least deformed of his efforts towards the cloud on a piece of tree bark. A wisp of purple mist curled forward and twined itself round the crust, which began to crumble away.

"Oh good," said the second voice. "That should keep me going until dinner."

"It's an example of the way that cookery is a prized skill on our planet," said Eddy, trying to make the best of the situation. "You may notice the two-colour effect of the pastry which is incredibly difficult to create and considered particularly delicious."

"Hmmmm," said the first voice. "I've tasted worse."

"Needs more salt," said the third.

"What's next?" said the first voice. "Second item."

"Is it pudding?" said the second voice. "That would be nice."

"Actually," said Eddy, "I'm afraid we had a bit of a problem. We were going to show you a picture. And an elephant. But…"

"Instead –" Millie produced a piece of paper from behind her back – "I've got a picture of a ephelant that I drawed." She tilted a bold, bright-crayoned picture towards the cloud. "Ephelants are brilliant. Also it is art. That is brilliant, too. Thank you." She curtsied.

"I did it when we got back from the zoo," she whispered to Eddy. "I had crayons and paper but it was a bit of a rush."

"Oh, dear," said the third voice. "No sense of form. The crudest handling of colour. And the technique – ghastly."

"Perhaps you are being a bit harsh," said the second voice. "If you look closely, does it not perhaps have a sort of innocent charm? Oh, no, you're right. It is terrible, isn't it? And what is it supposed to be? Six legs…"

"One is a trunk and one is its tail," said Millie.

"And what are these round things?" said the second voice. "Wheels?"

"They are its ears," said Millie. "You must be stupid if you don't know that."

"Well it's a very poor presentation so far," said the first voice. "Even allowing for your primitive nature and low intelligence. You are going to have to do much better with the third item."

The third item, thought Eddy. *What third item?*

An idea came into his head. Could he? Well, what did they have to lose?

"You know what?" said Eddy. "I am sick and tired of being told that we are stupid and useless, and that we're weird because we stick our food into our heads. Maybe we haven't got the biggest brains in the universe, but we've being doing alright with them so far. So I'll tell you what the third item is – it's us."

"Oh, dear," said the first voice.

"Human beings," Eddy continued. "Because we may not be perfect. We make mistakes and we get things wrong. But we do our best and we're funny and we dream our dreams and we try not to mess things up. And I reckon that makes us as special as you can get."

"Finished?" said the third voice.

"I hope so," said the second voice.

"That was one of the worst presentations I have ever seen," said the first voice. "It is quite clear that there is nothing special about this planet. It's not even as good as ordinary. The water is quite wasted on you. Much better to let the Malvalians have it and share it round the universe where it can do some good."

"And make them a vast profit," said Thursday.

"That's nothing to do with us," said the first voice.

"But—" said Eddy.

"But nothing," said the first voice. "You had your chance."

"Time for dinner," said the second voice. "I couldn't just have another of those pies before we go, could I? To tide me over."

"You've got a nerve," said Henry. He stuck his hand under his jumper and blew a loud, fruity armpit fart. "There's my answer."

"Go and have your dinner and I hope it makes you sick," said Eddy.

"One moment," said the first voice. "We want to hear that again."

"Which bit," said Eddy. "The part about being sick?"

"Not you," said the voice. "The one with the pie. What did you just do?"

"What, this?" said Henry. He stuck his hand up his jumper again, and let out another armpit fart.

"Extraordinary," said the first voice.

"Remarkable," said the third voice.

"That's nothing," said Henry, breaking into a quick burst of "Happy Birthday".

Muttering came from the purple cloud. Sparks of lightning flashed through it.

And then…

"Unique," said the second voice. "We know of no other creature in the entire universe that can make sound in that way. You do have a special ability after all."

"Does that mean Earth is saved?" said Eddy. "That you have changed your minds?"

"No, of course not," said the first voice. "This place is still a complete dump. However, we will recommend that as your species is of special interest, some of you are transferred to a space zoo before the planet is destroyed."

"A zoo?" said Eddy. "But we were in a place like that. We had to get away from it right at the start of all this."

"Well there you are, then," said the first voice. "Ask them if they will have you back. All sorted."

"And you had better get a move on," said the second voice. "I heard that the Malvalian pillaging fleet is on its way, and they are going to start extracting the water tomorrow."

And with that the purple cloud drifted apart and disappeared.

"They were not very nice," said Millie. "So what do we do now?"

PARP!

27

SORRY

"I'm sorry," said Eddy. "I've messed up. The painting.
The elephant. Everything."

"Hey," said Thursday, "you tried."

"And it wasn't good enough," said Eddy. "And now the
Malvalian fleet is arriving tomorrow to steal the water and
I don't know what to do next. But I'm not going back to
the cage on the Malvalian ship like the Council said we
should. I'm not running away in the podule and leaving
all my family and my friends here. Why wouldn't anyone
listen to us? Why do we have to do this on our own?"

"We're not on our own," said Thursday. "We're together.

All of us here. And maybe we can still think of a way to save the planet."

"Hurray!" said Millie.

"Though I have to warn you that no one has ever stopped a Malvalian Pillaging Fleet once it arrived," Thursday continued.

"That's not a great way to begin," said Henry.

"Then let's begin with what Drax has got everyone doing down in Tidemark Bay," said Eddy. "Professor – he's making people build a huge wall of shiny things around the harbour. You're a scientist. Have you any idea what it could be?"

"I suspect they are planning to use a hyper-energy pulse beam from their spacecraft," the Professor's voice boomed from Millie's stomach. "They need the reflecting wall round the harbour to focus its energy out onto the sea. The seawater would boil up into the air and form clouds, which the Malvalians would shrink and load into their cargo ships."

"What would happen if we tried to destroy the reflector wall?" said Eddy. "I suppose the Malvalians would just be able to fight us off. Space aliens always have mega-powered ray guns and laser torpedoes and stuff like that."

"No weapons on foreign planets," said Thursday. "It's against Intergalactic Law. And Malvalians don't break the law. They don't need to. Not when they can hypnotize their victims to do exactly what they want."

"So if we could destroy the reflector wall," said Eddy, "that would stop them. But we'd have to find a way to get past the guards. All those cats. All those claws."

"Sure you could stop them," said Thursday, "but only this time. They would just rebuild. A stronger wall. And more guards. The water is too valuable for them to fly away and leave it. Beating them once isn't enough. The only way they will give up is if they think they will never win. We have to make them believe they have lost before they start."

"We've got to come up with a plan," said Eddy.

"Huh. Plans," said Henry. "You know what they say about those. The best laid plans of mice and men often end up in a right old mess."

"Do mice make plans?" said Millie.

"You don't have to help," Eddy said to Henry. "If you don't think we will be able to come up with a way to save the planet."

"I'm just saying," said Henry. "Of course I'll help."

"Right," said Eddy. "We've got to work it out tonight. If we just try hard enough, I'm sure we can think of something."

★ ✿ ★

"I can't think of anything," said Eddy.

He was sitting in the podule surrounded by crumbs of burned pastry from the pies that had been supper. Henry sat next to him, occasionally playing snatches of tunes on his armpit. Thursday was halfway up a wall, hanging upside down. Millie lay dozing, hugging Horaceboris tight.

"I can't do this," Eddy said. He rubbed his eyes with the back of his hand. They were aching with tiredness. He wished he could sleep, but his brain was racing, trying to come up with a plan. Trying – but failing.

"It was hard enough having to take care of Millie," he said, "but trying to look after the whole world…it's too much!"

Millie stirred in her sleep.

"Hero Hound," she mumbled. "He'll help. Nothing can beat him."

"I wish," said Eddy. "But we all know he's just a story."

"Yes," said Henry. "Unless you are a Malvalian."

"What?" said Eddy.

"You remember," said Henry. "The Malvalians think everything on the telly is real. What was it you told them about Hero Hound? He's got superpowers and he's…"

"Strong and brave and nothing can stop him," said Eddy. "That's what they say at the end of the programme every week. Henry, you're a genius."

"No one's ever called me that before," said Henry.

"I bet," said Thursday. "What are you talking about?"

"Hero Hound," said Eddy. "He's a dog in a story. He fights baddies and he always wins. And the Malvalians think he's real. Well we're going to make him real. We're going to make them believe that they can never beat him."

He snatched up Millie's pad of paper and crayons. "We can make this work."

Eddy woke with a start. The sun was streaming in through the podule's windows.

Morning. He had sat late into the night, plotting with Henry, Thursday and the Professor (who had kept his voice down to avoid waking Millie), scribbling ideas and putting together a plan to stop the Malvalians, and make them believe that they would never be able to steal the Earth's water.

It was laid out in front of him now, written in coloured crayons. All eighteen steps of it. The plan had seemed clear last night, but this morning he wasn't so sure. He didn't know if it was too complicated. Or too difficult. Or too crazy. But one thing he did know – it was all they had.

SOFTY

"Here is all the money that I've got left from my Christmas present fund," Eddy said to Henry. "Your first job is to get down to Saltburn Sands and buy as much fish as you can. You should be able to get quite a lot with that cash. And remember, everybody, the Malvalian fleet is on its way today, so there is no time to lose."

"Got you," said Henry.

Eddy stuffed the last of the meat and potato pies into his backpack, pulled his Christmas bobble hat on, and headed off to Tidemark Bay, leaving Millie and Thursday in the podule.

It had rained hard in the night, and the

228

morning was bitingly cold. There was ice everywhere, which made Eddy's walk slow and treacherous.

"Lovely day," he lied to the cat patrol, as he reached the edge of the town.

There was no sign of any people. Everyone must already be at work down by the harbour. But the place was far from empty. There were cats everywhere, roaming freely, strolling down the middle of streets, and wandering in and out of houses where the doors had been left wide open.

He passed a short row of shops. There were cats in the window of the butcher's, chomping their way through a tray of steaks. And next door, in a clothes shop, a tabby was sitting on a fluffy pink jumper, happily kneading its paws and claws up and down and rapidly turning it into a pile of pink shreds.

Eddy made his way home and walked in through the unlocked front door. He pulled a piece of paper from his pocket – a list of things that he needed for the plan. The kitchen was the first stop. He found the fridge open, and a fat grey cat rolling around on the floor in front of it with a chicken leg. The cat looked up at him for a moment, then got back to business, chewing and tearing into its treat.

Eddy was about to shoo it out of the house, when he remembered that everyone else in Tidemark Bay was hypnotized, and no one was stopping the cats from doing what they wanted. He needed to pretend that he was just like them, or he would give himself away, so he left the cat alone and collected what he had written on his list:

```
KITCHEN -    Bottle of washing-up liquid
             Portable radio
             Pepper grinder
             Drinking straws
             Forks (6)
```

Then he went round the rest of the house, filling
his backpack.

```
BEDROOM - Alarm clock
          Bag of marbles
BATHROOM - 2 large towels
           Toothbrush
FRONT ROOM - Tinsel from Christmas decorations (lots)
             Sticky tape (in desk)
CUPBOARD UNDER STAIRS - Big spanners
                        Hero Hound costume from box of samples
                        Tennis ball
BACK GARDEN - Washing line
```

That was the easy part done. He took a deep breath.
Now for the hard bit. He went back out of the front
door and stepped carefully along the icy pavement to
the end of the street.

There was no sign of life at Clifftop Cottage. Eddy peered through the frosty railings of the high fence. The big dog must be around somewhere. Maybe if he made just a little noise. Nervously, he pushed the handle on the front gate. There was a faint creak as the latch shifted.

A second later Eddy jumped backwards as a huge black mass of paws and drool and snout hurled itself against the gate with an almighty thud. Eddy's heart was thumping as if it was trying to break out through his ribs.

Brutus stood on his hind legs, front paws against the gate, and looked down at Eddy.

"*Arf!*" he said.

"Hello, boy," said Eddy, his voice tense and tight and weedy. He reached over his shoulder into his backpack, and pulled out one of Henry's pies. "Look what I've got." He tossed the pie over the gate.

Brutus turned and pounced on it with a slavering grunt. The pie disappeared in one great mouthful, and the dog hurled himself at the gate again.

"*Arf!*" But this time he sounded less like he wanted to have Eddy for his main course. His mouth flopped open, slobbering tongue lolling over his yellowing teeth.

"Was that good?" said Eddy. "I bet a big boy like you

would like another one, wouldn't you?" He pulled a
second pie from his backpack. His hand trembled as
this time he reached forward and held it just out of
reach. The dog pushed his snout between the bars and
– UNGGGG! – snatched the pie, tossed his head back
and gulped it down.

"Arf!"

"You like these, don't you?"

Brutus's tail wagged. Eddy took out a third pie. He
put it down on the ground in front of him. Then very
slowly and very nervously he lifted the latch on the
gate.

Brutus bounded forward. The gate swung open and
clanged against the fence as the dog pushed through
and troughed down the pie. Then he looked up at Eddy,
opened his great jaws…and licked Eddy's hand.

"You're just a big softy, really, aren't you?" said Eddy.

"Arf!" Brutus agreed. His tail wagged again.

"I bet you would like a walk now, hey?"

Eddy pulled out the washing line, doubled it over
and slipped it through Brutus's collar. The dog bounded
along excitedly as Eddy led him back towards the
podule.

FISHY

> ## THE PLAN. STEP 2 -
> ### GET AS MANY CATS AS POSSIBLE
> ### AWAY FROM GUARDING THE HARBOUR

"Yes," said Henry. "I've got it. I go to Tidemark Bay with my bags of fish. My job is to keep as many cats as I can away from the big reflector wall in the harbour. On my way there, wherever I see a bunch of cats hanging around, I chuck them something from the bags to keep them busy. When I reach the harbour, I use the rest of the fish to lure the cat guards as far away as I can. Then I find a place to hide and wait for you to turn up."

"We're going to give you a thirty-minute start," said Eddy. "And you will need this." He wrapped a long strand of tinsel round and round Henry's head, and secured it to his ears with sticky tape. "To stop you getting hypnotized. Good luck. And be careful on that ice."

Eddy, Millie and Thursday watched Henry head off down the frozen pavement towards Tidemark Bay.

"And now we get ready for our part," said Eddy.

"*Arf!*" said Brutus. He had decided that these people who handed out pies were his new best friends. Millie fed him another one while Eddy fastened a Hero Hound cape round his chest. Thursday slipped a Hero Hound cap, packed with tinsel, over the dog's head, and tied its strap under his jaw. Eddy added the black eyemask that completed the costume. The famous pawprint logo glinted gold in the pale winter sunlight.

"He looks just like on the TV," said Millie. "It's Hero Hound – he's superpowered and strong and brave and absolutely nothing can stop him."

"And that's exactly what the Malvalians are going to think," said Eddy.

"I gotta hand it to you, kid, it's a clever plan," said Thursday. "As long as it works, of course. Otherwise it's just complicated and crazy."

"It will work," said Eddy. "It's got to work. Hats on, Millie. It's time to go."

Henry had almost competed his journey
through Tidemark Bay. All along the way, the
smell of the fish that he was carrying had
attracted groups of cats. He had hurled handfuls
of haddock and hake and herrings to them, and left them
spitting and spatting over the best bits as he passed on
down the road.

Now he was approaching the harbour by a narrow
back alley, keeping out of sight of any guards on lookout
duty. He spread the last of his fish out in front of a
wooden fence, then crept through the shadows
towards the great wall of mirrors and shiny
objects. There were cats everywhere, prowling round
the harbour, while the people of Tidemark Bay carried
shiny objects to the final bare patch in the wall.

Ducking into a doorway, Henry pulled a
pair of kippers out of his jacket pocket,
and waved them above his head, like a
cheerleader with a whiffy pair of pompoms. The
nearest cats looked round, noses twitching, then started
to walk towards him to find the source of the smell.
More cats followed, and more, until every cat stationed

236

by the reflector wall left its post in search
of food. As the leading cats drew near Henry
threw the kippers back towards the fish that he
had spread out. The wave of animals rushed past him,
and pounced on the offering.

Henry turned round to watch the harbour,
ignoring the squabbling and squalling
behind him, and waiting for Eddy to arrive.

Give a cat a fish, and you feed it for a meal.

Show a cat a man with bags full of fish, and it will
follow him in search of seconds.

Behind Henry's back, cats that he had fed on his way
through town were piling over the wooden fence into
the alley, cats who had sniffed out his route and come
looking for more, joining the crowd that had been
tempted away from the reflector wall. Unseen by
Henry, fifty cats became a hundred, the hundred
became two hundred and kept growing.

Eddy's plan had been to get as many cats as possible
away from the harbour. But instead, all it had done was
to attract every cat in town towards it. They polished
off the last of their meal, then sat and stared at
Henry with greedy eyes.

30

ICY

THE PLAN. STEP 3 -
EDDY AND BRUTUS CHASE OFF ANY REMAINING CATS AND KEEP DRAX BUSY. HENRY, THURSDAY AND MILLIE SNEAK TO THE REFLECTOR WALL AND USE THE SPANNERS TO UNDO THE BOLTS HOLDING THE SCAFFOLDING TOGETHER.

Brutus tugged at the washing line that was acting as his lead, eagerly following his nostrils towards the great smell of cat. The other end of the cord was wrapped securely round Eddy's left hand. The big dog was far too powerful to pull back, and either didn't know or didn't care what the command "Heel!" meant. Eddy was being dragged along, sometimes at a trot, and sometimes with his feet sliding over the icy pavement. Thursday and Millie, who was clutching her favourite cuddly

Horaceboris, could only just keep up.

As they neared the harbour, Eddy signalled to Millie. The little girl filled her lungs, opened her mouth and bellowed, *"Yaaayyyy! It's Hero Hound! He's superpowered and strong and brave and absolutely nothing can stop him!"*

"That little lady is loud!" said Thursday.

"You should hear it from where I am," Professor Blubblubblabblubblubblubblap rumbled from inside Millie. "I've known exploding comets that made less noise."

They rounded the last corner. Now they could see the harbour, and the crowd of people gathered by the reflector wall.

"Look!" Eddy panted as Brutus dragged him on. "No cats. Henry has done a brilliant job. He's got them all out of the way. All we've got to do is keep Drax occupied so the others can get to the reflector wall without him noticing."

And there up ahead, in the feline form of Ginger Tom, was Drax G'varglestarg, sprawled fast asleep on the silver cube of his communications interface in the middle of the High Street.

Brutus didn't care about names. Or space aliens in artificial bodies. As far as he was concerned, it was just a cat. And Brutus knew what cats were for. Cats were for chasing.

Barking loudly, he set off across the frozen ground, paws skittering on the slippery surface as he accelerated towards his target. Eddy skidded and slithered along behind him on the end of his lead.

This was the moment that Henry had been waiting for. He broke cover from the shadows of the alleyway and headed for the reflector wall, a set of spanners clanking in his trouser pockets.

"Come on!" he yelled to Millie and Thursday.

The two hundred cats in the alley behind him took this as their cue. Cat logic said that if the man with the fish was moving, it must surely be to get more fish to feed to them. They chased after Henry and surrounded him, mewing and pawing and pleading and forming a barrier that completely blocked his path. He couldn't take a step without tripping over the tangle of furry bodies. And neither could Millie or Thursday. There was no way that they could follow the plan to get to the reflector wall and start undoing the bolts that held it together.

Step three of the plan was starting to go wrong.

Back in the High Street, Drax G'varglestarg was still fast asleep and blissfully unaware of the huge dog that was rapidly bearing down on him. Brutus took one last bound and launched himself at his target. As he did so, he barked out a mighty "ARF!" that ruffled Drax's whiskers and woke him with a start. Seeing the slavering open jaws heading his way, Drax leaped straight upwards with every ounce of bounce he could find in his legs. He was just in time. Brutus's mouth snapped shut on empty air.

Bounce over, Drax came straight back down again and landed on the dog's head. Front paws on Brutus's ears and back paws on his snout, he dug in for a firm grip. The dog yelped as claws found soft flesh and sank deep. Drax clung on, hugging tight to the dog's head and covering his eyes, so that all Brutus could see was a curtain of fur. Surprised, in pain, and with no idea where he was going, there was only one thing for Brutus to do.

He went bonkers, charging round in circles trying to shake his unwelcome passenger off his head. Behind him, Eddy still had hold of the makeshift lead. He wished he hadn't wrapped it round his hand quite so many times to make sure he had a firm grip, because having a firm grip no longer seemed like a good idea. As Brutus turned and twisted, Eddy felt himself losing his footing on the icy ground. His feet flailed around for a moment, and then he fell flat on his back.

"Owwww!" he shouted. His cries mixed with the dog's howling and Drax's yowling, as he was dragged helplessly up and down the frozen street like a human sledge.

Step three had really gone right off the rails. But it had one more nasty surprise in store.

As Eddy was dragged along, his hat came off.

His head was suddenly full of the recorded message that was coming from the communications interface.

"IT'S A LOVELY DAY," it said. "EVERYTHING IS NORMAL. BUILD THE REFLECTOR WALL." It was Drax's voice. The voice that he had heard way back in the woods the first time he and Millie had seen the podule. The voice that had taken control of everyone in Tidemark Bay. And Eddy knew that very soon it would take control of him, too.

MOUSY

> **THE PLAN. STEP 4 _**
> **USE TOWELS AND STICKY TAPE TO WRAP...**

But it didn't matter what step four of Eddy's plan was. Or steps five to eighteen, come to that. They were in no position to do anything. Henry, Millie and Thursday were surrounded by cats, and couldn't get near the reflector wall. Eddy was even more helpless, being dragged around the ice on his back, with an alien voice slowly taking over his mind. It looked like things just couldn't get any worse.

And then they did.

Brutus, who couldn't see where he was going because Drax was over his eyes, ran slap bang into a lamp post. Drax jumped out of the way at the last moment and

clambered up the pole, and Brutus took the blow full
on his head. He staggered woozily.

Eddy slithered across the frozen High Street towards
him, and arrived just as the dog gave up the battle to
stay on his feet. Brutus collapsed in a daze right on top
of Eddy, pinning him to the ground.

Eddy could still hear Drax's voice in the recorded
commands coming through the communications
interface.

"IT'S A LOVELY DAY," the voice repeated. "BUILD
THE REFLECTOR WALL." He could feel it starting to
work on him. His legs twitched to get moving, but
Brutus was too heavy for him to shift. Eddy was going
nowhere.

So that was it, Eddy just managed to think over the
voice in his head. The plan to make the Malvalians
think that they could never beat Hero Hound, the plan
to make them give up and go home,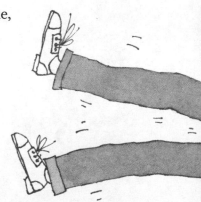
the plan to save the water and the
planet – all over. They had lost.
Earth had lost.

It looked like what Henry had
said was turning out to be true.

The best laid plans of mice and men really did often end up in a right old mess.

Although, in fact, it was a bit too early to judge how the mouse's plan had worked out.

The mouse in question was hiding in a burger box in the gutter just across the street from where Eddy was lying. It had found the box in the early hours of the morning when the streets were empty. And it had also found what was left of the burger, polished it off, got indigestion, and decided to take a nap while its meal went down. When it woke up hours later ready to head for home, it was horrified to find the street crawling with cats, and decided to sit tight while it worked out what to do.

After a long think, it had come up with a plan. It wasn't a very good plan, but if you are expecting something more complicated, you've probably got the wrong idea about mouse intelligence. This was the plan, in its entirety: *Run for it.*

The mouse peeped cautiously out from the burger box.

The cats seemed to have gone. This was the moment to put the plan into action.

It was also the moment when Drax G'varglestarg jumped down from the lamp post to find out just who had tried to cause him trouble. Who had managed to get this far without being hypnotized – and how? He peered at the figure lying on the floor. It was no good – they all looked alike to him.

Eddy peered back. He had run out of ideas.

"Please," he said. "Don't take the water."

"How do you know about the water?" Drax's voice thumped into Eddy's head over the message that everything was lovely. "Wait. You?" His eyes narrowed. "I can't imagine how you managed to get back here. But I obviously made a mistake when I didn't deal with you in the first place. Still, that's easily put right."

"What do you mean?" said Eddy out loud. "You're not allowed to use weapons on another planet."

"I don't need weapons," said Drax. "I've got a town full of people and two hundred cats who will do the job for me." Drax's voice boomed between Eddy's ears. "INSTRUCTION FOR ALL TUBEOIDS AND ALL CATS..."

And at that very second, the mouse counted down –

which in mouse numbers went *lots...some...a...none* – and made its run for safety. It streaked across the High Street, and into the corner of Drax's vision. Drax's head snapped to one side to follow it. The cat instincts buried in his body rose to the surface irresistibly. One thought and one thought only filled Drax's mind.

CATCH THE MOUSE!

And one thought and one thought only was transmitted as an instruction to a town full of people and two hundred cats.

"...CATCH THE MOUSE!"

Drax twisted round and flailed a paw. The mouse swerved wildly out of reach.

Two hundred cats turned away from Henry and the hope of more fish, ears pricked, and charged up the High Street, mewing wildly.

Around the harbour people dropped the metal objects that they were carrying and hurried away from the reflector wall, muttering, "Catch the mouse! *Catch the mouse!*"

The middle of the High Street was soon filled with a wriggling scrum of cats and people, arms grabbing and legs scrambling.

"What is happening?" said Millie.

"I have no idea," said Thursday. "But Eddy's in the middle of that mayhem. We'd better get him out of there."

Henry picked Millie up and pushed through the crowd towards Eddy, past yowling cats and people shouting "Have you seen it?" and "Mind my foot!" and "It's over there!" – even though the mouse had already slipped unseen out of the edge of the crowd and scurried away to safety.

"STOP!" Eddy could hear Drax in his head. The Malvalian had clearly managed to overcome his urge to chase the mouse. "BACK TO WORK! EVERYTHING IS NORMAL!"

People started to split away from the mouse hunt.

Henry put Millie down by the lamp post, and strained to lift Brutus off Eddy. The dog slowly staggered to its feet and shook his head. Then he saw the crowd in front of him, and leaped into it, barking enthusiastically and scattering cats in all directions.

"Back to work!" said Eddy, scrabbling to get up. "Everything is normal."

"Whoah!" Thursday grabbed hold of him with most of his legs. "You stay right where you are."

Eddy struggled to break free.

Millie picked up Eddy's bobble hat.

"So," she asked him, "is the plan working?"

32

GIGGLY

-Ha-ha!-
-Ho-ho!-
-Tee-hee!-
-Heh-heh-heh!-
-Ha-ha!-
-Tee-hee!-

"Is it going well?" Millie added. "Are we winning?"

And then a very strange thing happened.

Henry laughed.

He had carefully studied all eighteen stages of Eddy's plan, and learned exactly what he had to do. He had watched it collapse almost instantly into confusion and chaos. He'd seen Eddy dragged flat on his back along the ice by a howling dog with a cat stuck on its head. He'd been mobbed by hundreds of fish-crazy cats. He'd seen a crowd of people scrambling together like wild animals. He was now watching Eddy try to break free of Thursday's grip so he could join in with building the reflector wall. Their whole plan had gone about as wrong as wrong could be. And now, when Millie asked her wide-eyed question, he could think of no other answer.

He laughed. For the first time since the Malvalians had taken him prisoner so long ago. All those years without even a smile. And now the dam burst, and it all came flooding out. He laughed and laughed till tears ran down his cheeks and he bent double, gasping for breath.

"Are – we – winning?" he panted. And then he started laughing again.

The sound rang through Eddy's head. Drax's voice, the voice that was telling him to build the reflector wall, started to break up, like a badly tuned radio. All he could hear was Henry laughing. And then his own jaw started to wobble. It was all such a shambles. He broke into laughter, too. Laughter that completely drowned out Drax.

Some of the people around him started to giggle.

"I can't hear Drax any more," said Eddy, through snorts of laughter. "I don't need my hat. The laughter is blocking him out."

"How very interesting," said Professor Blubblubblabblubblubblubblap from Millie's stomach. "It must be breaking up your normal brain patterns. It's not something I have ever been able to study, of course. Laughter is beyond my experience."

"There's not much humour out in the galaxy, you know, kid," said Thursday. "And none at all among the Malvalians. They probably never came across it before."

"Which means they won't know how to deal with it," said Eddy.

He looked around. Laughter was spreading through the crowd. And everywhere it passed there were puzzled faces as minds began to shake off the Malvalian control.

"We can beat them!" chuckled Eddy. "We can break the hypnosis. All we have to do is get everyone laughing."

"We should find my daddy," said Millie. "He knows loads of jokes. Even some funny ones."

"And mine does, too," said Eddy. "They must be in this crowd somewhere."

The laughter around them was getting quieter now.

Drax's message was coming through the communications interface more clearly again. "Build the reflector wall."

"We need to find them fast," said Eddy.

It didn't take long to drag them out of the crowd. They both looked confused.

"What?" said Eddy's dad. "Where?"

"I don't understand," said Uncle Ken. "We were just…"

"Jokes," said Eddy. "We need you to tell jokes. Keep this crowd laughing."

Eddy's dad perked up.

"Jokes," he said. "Well, you've got the right man."

"You certainly have," said Uncle Ken. "And your dad's here as well." He chuckled. A few heads turned.

"Let's see who can get them going best then," said Uncle Ken.

"You're on," said Eddy's dad.

In the next few minutes, chickens crossed roads, ducks borrowed library books, sailors were washed up on desert islands, horses walked into pubs, goldfish drove tanks, and parrots gave away secrets. Drax's hold on the people of Tidemark Bay was completely broken as giggles and chuckles and chortles bellowed and billowed around the High Street.

The laughter would have been a lot less enthusiastic if the people had known what was going on directly above Tidemark Bay. It looked like a faint ripple that ran across half the sky through the grey clouds that cloaked the day.

But it wasn't a ripple. It was the Malvalian Grand Control ship, as big as a city, hidden behind its disguise shield.

And Malvalian Grand Control was not happy.

Drax G'varglestarg, who had taken refuge from the chaotic mouse hunt on the roof of the nearby Penguin Fish Restaurant, was trying to explain what had happened. Yes, he had lost his power over the minds of the local population. No, he could not say why, but it seemed to be connected to that weird squeaky coughing noise they had all started making. No, he didn't know what that was, but perhaps it was a sign that they were all ill.

And then it got really tricky for him.

"We have visual contact," said Grand Control. "We have a sighting of Hero Hound – repeat, Hero Hound.

We believe that he is responsible for the problem. Report."

"That's just a local life-form in a costume," Drax reported. "There is no Hero Hound. He's made up."

"That is not what the databank says," Grand Control replied. "The databank says that Hero Hound has amazing superpowers and nothing can stop him. Report."

"The databank is wrong."

"That's not what the databank says. The databank says that the databank is correct."

"It doesn't matter what it says about Hero Hound," Drax told Grand Control. "And it doesn't matter that I have lost control of the population. We don't need them any more. The reflector wall is ninety-seven per cent complete and perfectly operational."

Across the street, Thursday's antennae were twitching. He swivelled them round and – "Hey! I got a signal coming through. It sounds like the Malvalian fleet has arrived. And – uh-oh! You're not going to like what I'm hearing, kid."

What he was hearing was Drax's voice:

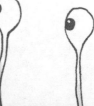

259

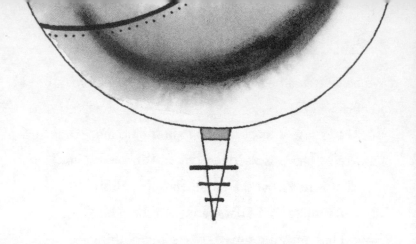

"ACTIVATE THE

HYPER-ENERGY PULSE BEAM
AND BEGIN UPLOADING
WATER NOW. THE PLAN
WILL STILL WORK."

FLUFFY

It was that word again. *Plan.* Just asking for trouble.

And round the corner trouble lumbered, tall, grey-blue and absolutely enormous in the bottom department, ready to prove that it's not only the plans of mice and men that go wrong, but ones thought up by space aliens as well.

The Fluffy Wuffy Cushion Bunny had got bored with squashing bushes and trees, and had left the woods in search of some variety to spice up its life. Its shambling steps had led it into Tidemark Bay, where it had been delighted to discover that cars made a lovely loud twanging noise when you sat on them, just before the wheels collapsed. Not to mention the crisp crunch they made just after the wheels collapsed. It couldn't decide which of those two sounds it liked more, so had to make them lots of times to see if it could pick a favourite.

As far as the Fluffy Wuffy Cushion Bunny was concerned, twangy things and crunchy things were both pretty good, but what it loved most of all were shiny things. And now in front of it was the biggest shiny thing it had ever seen in its life – a great wall of shine running right round the harbour.

And just as Thursday picked up Malvalian Grand Control transmitting the ominous words "Priming the hyper-energy pulse beam generator", the Fluffy Wuffy Cushion Bunny arrived at one end of the reflector wall. It turned, shimmied its massive rear, and plonked it down on a particularly fine nineteenth-century mantelpiece mirror in an elaborate golden frame. The bottom passed straight through, and slammed down on the wall's scaffold support. The scaffold buckled. That section of the reflector wall toppled forward and splashed into the waters of the harbour.

The collapse spread along the wall like a Mexican wave, taking the entire structure down. Half the shiny objects of Tidemark Bay were now actually *in* Tidemark Bay, and fast sinking to the bottom.

The chuckling crowd of people seemed to think that this was all part of some hilarious stunt, and laughed even more.

"Hyper-energy pulse beam generator primed," said the voice of Malvalian Grand Control. "Firing in five... four—"

"WAIT," said Drax. "We have a problem. The reflector wall is damaged."

"Can we still fire?" said Grand Control. "What percentage is damaged?"

"Rough estimate," said Drax. "A hundred. Ish."

"Assessing mission status," said Grand Control. "Reflector wall is destroyed. Local inhabitants have developed resistance to mind control. Hero Hound is operative. Estimated probability of success of this mission – zero. Estimated probability of success of attempting this mission again – zero. Mission is terminated. All units are ordered to abandon this planet and return to Malvalia. Repeat – all units return to Malvalia. Agent Ginger Tom report for disciplinary hearing. Mission has failed."

"They've given up!" said Thursday. "They're going home and they are not coming back. We won, kid!

They are not going to take the water – not now, not ever."

"We did it!" shouted Eddy. And then he and Henry and Thursday and Millie shared a well-earned moment of cheering and hugging and jumping up and down and shouting their heads off. Even Brutus came arfing over with his tail wagging.

"There's just one problem," said Eddy. "Drax is still on the loose somewhere. He's not going to be happy that we beat him. And his communications interface is over there. We can't keep everyone laughing for ever. He could take over people's minds again and get them to do something terrible in revenge for losing. I won't be happy till we've stopped that interface working."

"Actually, kid," said Thursday, "you got two problems. And the other one is heading right this way."

The Fluffy Wuffy Cushion Bunny had heaved itself up off the ground, and was lumbering towards them, ready to sit on anything and anyone.

"How," said Eddy, "do you stop one of those things?"

"Easy," said the Professor, "have you got a spatial matrix containment mine to hand?"

"Not only have I not got one," said Eddy, "I haven't the first idea what one is."

"I see," said the Professor. "Then I'm afraid that you really have got a problem."

To understand what happened next, it is important to know that the Malvalians had originally captured the Fluffy Wuffy Cushion Bunny to try to discover how to control its brain. The Malvalians still hadn't discovered how its brain worked, because although they had used X-rays and ultrasound scanners, and even a gigantic machine designed to pick up the Fluffy Wuffy Cushion Bunny, turn it upside down and shake it around a lot to see if anything fell out of its ear, they couldn't find a brain in the creature's head at all. In short, it was not the brightest alien in the galaxy.

As the Fluffy Wuffy Cushion Bunny advanced threateningly towards Eddy and his group, it caught sight of Millie holding her cuddly Horaceboris. Apart from being ten times smaller, Horaceboris looked remarkably like a Fluffy Wuffy Cushion Bunny – lumpy blue-grey body, a wide mouth, boggling eyes, and a shock of orange hair. So when it caught sight of Horaceboris, the Fluffy Wuffy Cushion Bunny used all its insignificant intellect to think as follows:

That blue-grey thing looks just like me.

I am very large, so that blue-grey thing must be very large, too.

The creature dressed in pink that is holding it is much bigger than it is.

So the creature dressed in pink that is holding it must also be much bigger than me.

Bigger things like to sit on smaller things.

If I get too close to the creature dressed in pink, it will sit on me.

So I must go the other way.

The podule I got out of is the other way.

So I must go back to the podule.

And it turned and shambled off.

The crowd of people clearly thought that this was the end of the show, though none of them were quite sure just what the show had been. They began to break up into small groups and wander off, chuckling and smiling to themselves.

"It's going away," said Eddy. "So that's one problem we don't need to worry about right now. Let's see about that communications interface." He walked over to the silver cube and picked it up. "I know I can stop it working by taking out the sieve in a sock – I mean the hemispherical perforated whatever it was. I just have to get into it.

"Open up," he said. "I'm a level nine and I order you to open."

But nothing happened. He rubbed his hands over it. He could still feel patches of the level nine slime on his fingers. But still the communications interface would not open.

"I don't get it," said Eddy. "The lid opened straight away for Drax."

"You probably need the mission code," said Professor Blubblubblabblubblubblubblap. "The Malvalians usually use a six-letter password."

"Only six letters," said Eddy. "That shouldn't take too long to crack."

"Their alphabet has 242 letters," the Professor added. "That's over two hundred million million combinations. To run through them all at ten a second would take me approximately six hundred and fifty thousand of your years."

"That's a bit too long," said Millie.

"We could hit it with something heavy," said Henry.

"It is designed to withstand the worst that interstellar travel can dish out," said the Professor. "Radiation, extremes of temperature, particle storms, space nits. I don't think that bashing it with a brick is going to work."

"Millie," said Eddy, "while we're trying to think of a way to open it, why don't you have a little play with it?"

"Okay," said Millie. She picked it up and twirled it round. "What does it do? Is it bouncy? No. Does it fly? No. Can it – oh, no it can't. What's this bit for? I think it's meant to…oh…"

There was a clang as a chunk of the casing fell off the communications interface. And a clatter as bits of its innards spilled out.

"It did break," said Millie.

"It may have been built to stand up to space travel," said Eddy. "But a minute in the hands of a four year old..."

"Four and three-quarters, thank you," said Millie. "And I did not break it. But what would happen if somebody had?"

"Somebody," said Eddy, "would be a total star."

"I did break it," said Millie. "I did! I did!"

From somewhere past one hundred thousand miles away, a message was directed at the broken interface.

"Grand Control to Ginger Tom. Can you hear me, Ginger Tom? Can you hear me, Ginger Tom?"

But he couldn't. Nobody could.

RAINY

They found Drax back at Eddy's house. He was sitting next to the computer.

I saw what you did to my communications interface.
I have no other options.
I surrender._

"We're sending you back," said Eddy. "We've got a podule waiting in the woods."

I can't go back, Drax typed. I have failed. Failure is not tolerated._

"You can't stay here," said Eddy.

"I will have him," said Millie. "I have always wanted a cat."

"What if your mum and dad don't agree?" said Eddy.

"Don't be silly," said Millie. "They always agree. In the end."

Drax G'varglestarg contemplated the future. A future of three meals a day, sleeping in the sun, being waited on by humans, and having all the time he wanted to further his researches into small furred and feathered creatures.

No work, lots of rest, servants who got things done. That sounded good. In fact, it sounded pretty much like the Malvalian way of life. Okay – he would be Ginger Tom from now on.

I accept,_ he typed.

"And I will call you Mr Furrytummysnugglepaws,"
said Millie.

On one condition. Drax added. I will meet you halfway:
Furrytummy or Snugglepaws. Not both.

"Snugglepaws," said Millie.
"*Mr* Snugglepaws."

"Thursday, Professor,"
said Eddy. "I guess it's time
to say goodbye. You can use
the podule."

"I think I want to go with
them," said Henry. "Back into space."

"What?" said Eddy. "Why?"

"I miss Ethel," said Henry. "And she's out
there with the Malvalian fleet. We were together
for a long time."

"Just give me a second," said Eddy. "Professor…"
He whispered something in Millie's ear as he led her
out of the room.

They came back a few minutes later. Eddy was
carrying the portable radio that he had put in his

backpack as part of his plan. He handed it to Henry.

"A present," he said.

"Ta," said Henry. "But I don't think it will be much use where I'm going."

"Just try it," said Eddy.

Henry turned it on.

"How are you today?" said a familiar voice.

"Ethel!" said Henry.

"I got the Professor to tell me how to do it," said Eddy.

"A simple modification using the memory and voice processor from the communications interface," said the Professor.

"She's got just the same databanks as the one on the Malvalian ship," said Eddy. "So she remembers you and all the time you had together."

"It's so good to hear you again," said Henry. "I can stay here on Earth now. Come on, let's find an oven and bake some pies. I reckon we can crack it together."

"It's time we went," said Thursday.

"Indeed," said the Professor. "But first I need to get out of this body. I shall almost be sorry to leave it. One has encountered so many theories about what might go on inside a tubeoid, so to actually be in here has been fascinating, surprising, and quite, quite ghastly. You shall be the subject of a detailed scientific book, young lady. And your innards have also given me a very exciting idea for an absolutely terrifying and disgusting theme park ride."

"Ooh!" said Millie. "My tummy is going to be famous!"

"So," said the Professor, "where is the exit from these tubes?"

"I can think of an obvious way out," said Eddy. "You can flow anywhere in Millie's body, yes?"

"Indeed," said the Professor.

"Right," said Eddy. "We'll need a bowl to catch you in."

"I can't," Millie said, ten minutes later.

"Yes you can," said Eddy. "Try harder."

"I am trying harder," said Millie. "I'm thinking of really sad things but nothing is making me cry. You'll have to help me."

"Um...pony in a snowstorm," said Eddy.

"That's not sad," said Millie. "That is cute."

"Kitten with a bandage on its paw."

"No."

"Your friend Sophie," said Eddy, "in a princess dress much prettier than yours."

"Nooooooooooooo!" Millie's bottom lip wobbled.
"Waaaaaaaaaaaa!"

And the Professor flowed down her face as tears.

They found a clean jam jar with a tight-fitting lid for the Professor to travel in. Eddy carried him into the woods, with Thursday and Millie walking beside him.

The Fluffy Wuffy Cushion Bunny was already sitting by the podule.

"Podule. Open doors," said Eddy.

At the sight of Millie, the big blue-grey beast scrambled into the cargo hold.

"This is going to be my last order," Eddy said. "I want you to transport that creature back to his home planet. And then take these two wherever they want to go."

"You got it," said the podule. "Sir."

"So long, kids," said Thursday. "It's been a gas."

"With all that water, don't you mean it's been a liquid?" said the Professor.

"That," said Eddy, "was almost a joke. Keep at it."

Life round Tidemark Bay soon returned to normal. Almost.

Maxton Banderfield decided to forgive Eddy for destroying his painting. It had never been one of his favourites, and besides, he'd had a sudden mysterious burst of inspiration and decided to stop painting the sea and start doing horses instead.

Sergeant Constable found his perfect shed (thatched-cottage look, with matching wishing well) and discovered that he didn't miss the police station at all.

The one odd thing was the way that nobody in Tidemark Bay could quite remember what had happened for three days. Everyone's memory was very fuzzy. All they had to go on was a lot of flat cars and a mysterious lack of shiny metal objects.

Until the local news blog came out the next day.

ESCAPED ELEPHANT TERRORIZES TOWN

RUNAWAY JUMBO DAMAGES POLICE STATION, TRAMPLES CARS, AND DESTROYS COMMUNITY SCULPTURE PROJECT AT LOCAL HARBOUR.

Eddy read the story eagerly. It was, he thought, a brilliantly written piece of investigative reporting. Especially as there was barely a single correct fact in it.

But the people of Tidemark Bay lapped it up. It explained everything. They had been building something down at the harbour, hadn't they? And that big grey-blue thing that some of them could vaguely remember must have been an elephant because – well, what else could it possibly have been?

Eddy stood in the front garden, looking out into the night. They had saved the water and saved the world, and no one would ever know, apart from him and Millie and Henry.

And that was okay.

Clouds covered the moon. Rain was falling steadily. He wondered where his friends Thursday and the Professor were now.

"Eddy?" his mother was calling from the front door. "What are you doing out there with no coat? You're getting soaked."

Eddy tilted his head back and let the rain splash on his face.

"I know," he said. "It's brilliant."

A Bit of the Universe
(not quite to scale)

G Force Scale
3G : Feeling Heavy
4G : Can't Move
5G : Squashed Flat!
SPEEDO : WEEEEEEEE!

Mars

Podule

the Moon

Tidemark Bay

CZ492
Gamma
[the Earth]

A SELECTION OF THE JOKES THAT PREVENTED THE WORLD FROM ENDING...

What do cows read in the morning?

Moospapers.

What is big, grey and wears glass slippers?

Cinderelephant.

What did 0 say to number 8?

Nice belt.

A penguin walks up to a policeman and says, "Excuse me, I've lost my brother. Have you seen him?" The policeman says, "I don't know. What does he look like?"

What do you give to an itchy pig?

Oinkment.

What did the fish say when it swam into the wall?

Dam.

Why did the duck cross the road?

It was the chicken's day off.

What's the difference between a guitar and a fish?

You can't tuna fish.

What is white and sweet and swings from tree to tree?

A meringue-utan.

Where do injured insects go?

To the Waspital.

Why don't polar bears eat penguins?

They can't get the wrappers off.

What happened when the frog's car broke down?

It got toad away.

What do you call Superman when he's lost his powers?

Man.

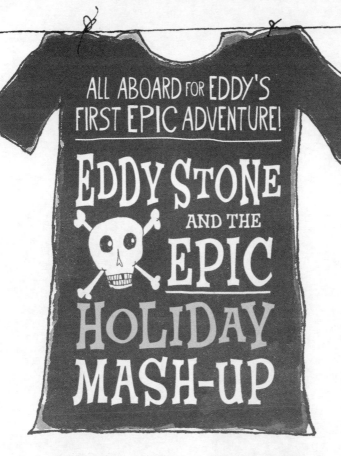

ALL ABOARD FOR EDDY'S
FIRST EPIC ADVENTURE!

EDDY STONE
AND THE
EPIC
HOLIDAY
MASH-UP

WHEN EDDY FINDS A PIRATE IN HIS
GRAN'S BATH, HIS MISERABLE SUMMER
HOLIDAY TURNS INTO A TREASURE HUNT.

Setting sail in a ship-shaped shed,
crewed by an old lady and a grumpy penguin,
what could possibly stop them?

ISBN: 9781474903059
www.usborne.com/fiction

ABOUT THE AUTHOR

Simon Cherry is an experienced television producer, writer and director who worked in Melvyn Bragg's Arts Department at ITV for almost twenty years. Simon lives in Surrey with his wife, two teenage sons and their ginger cat, James, who likes three meals a day exactly on time, and a choice of beds for naps. *Eddy Stone* is Simon's first series for children.

To James - Ginger Cat and
Rightful Ruler of the House.
SC

For Oscar Sudbery - With a
Special mention to Felix, who might
have fun reading it to him!
FB

First published in the UK in 2016 by Usborne Publishing Ltd., Usborne House,
83-85 Saffron Hill, London EC1N 8RT, England. www.usborne.com

Text copyright © Simon Cherry, 2016
The right of Simon Cherry to be identified as the author of this work has been
asserted by him in accordance with the Copyright, Designs and Patents Act, 1988.

Illustrations copyright © Usborne Publishing Ltd., 2016
Illustrations by Francis Blake.

The name Usborne and the devices 🏆🌐 are Trade Marks of Usborne Publishing Ltd.

A CIP catalogue record for this book is available from the British Library.

JFMAMJJA OND /16

ISBN 9781474903448 03906/1
Printed in the UK.